Resolving
DALTON
JONES

A NOVEL BY
ALBERT BRYCE HANNER

FIRST EDITION
Printed in the United States of America

Printed by CreateSpace
4900 Lacross Rd
North Charleston, SC 29406, USA
www.createspace.com

To my wife Jessica, and kids;
Maya, and Albert Monroe

"I just finished your book, thank you for letting me read it. I laughed, I cried, I pondered. It reads very well, easy, and smooth. I like your characters. I wanted you to explain them sooner—but after reading it I understand why you didn't. I am very proud of you. Love you."

– Aunt Patty Goodell
Flint, MI, 2012

"Every living creature is subject to the evils of sickness, old age, and death, and to the sadness that comes when his loved ones are stricken by these ills. These inevitable occasions of unhappiness constitute the problem of life."

– E.A. Burtt, *The Teachings of the Compassionate Buddha, page 28, ©1958.*

In loving memory

Patty Lynn Goodell
October 12, 1954 – July 9, 2013

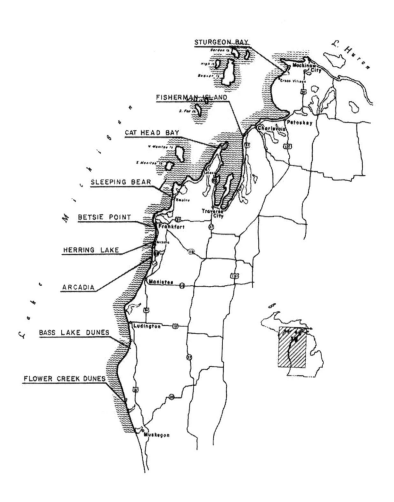

STURGEON BAY

FISHERMAN ISLAND

CAT HEAD BAY

SLEEPING BEAR

BETSIE POINT

HERRING LAKE

ARCADIA

BASS LAKE DUNES

FLOWER CREEK DUNES

L. Huron

L a k e   M i c h i g a n

Mackinaw City
Cross Village
Petoskey
Charlevoix
Traverse City
Frankfort
Arcadia
Manistee
Ludington
Muskegon

I wish to acknowledge my wife Jessica Marie Hanner, Craig Olson, Chris Ashton, my brothers Bob Hanner and Ryan Hanner, Colin Erickson, and Tim Shonsey for their reviews, edits, and constructive critiques during this long creative process.

Also an acknowledgment of the Michigan Department of Natural Resources for their conservation of such places as the *Leelanau State Park* and the *Grand Traverse Lighthouse*—where this story began.

—ABH

WHO IS DALTON JONES?

The published works of Dalton Jones...

Broken People (1968) ☆☆☆☆☆
"The author Dalton Jones is an amazing and triumphant new voice of this generation!"

Lonely Man (1970) ☆☆☆
"Dalton Jones has left us with a lack-luster sequel to last years best seller. In this instance, less was more."

Unrefined (1974) ☆☆
"Dalton Jones's third novel is poignant—but slow. His compassion and clarity of prose makes his protagonists sorrow our own—but overall doesn't measure up."

Return of the Lonely Man (1976) ☆☆☆☆
"Dalton Jones' writing is superior entertainment, and with each novel becomes something more serious and worthy of his exceptional talent."

Going East (1984) ☆☆☆☆
"Dalton Jones has evolved as a writer. *Going East* is a magnificent must read!"

Lonely Man Goes Home (1999) ☆☆☆☆☆

"One of America's great literary treasures is back! Here in *Lonely Man Goes Home,* Dalton Jones' first novel in fifteen years, he will surprise and delight you with the continuing adventures of our most loved protagonist."

Snap Shots (2003) ☆☆☆☆

"Ever since writing 1968's *Broken People,* Dalton Jones has produced a steady stream of profound American literature! "

This Life (2007) ☆☆☆☆

"A fine new collection of short stories that revisits some of Dalton Jones' most beloved characters from the last thirty-five years! This is a rich and satisfying collection."

The Problem of Life (2010) ☆☆☆☆☆

"Dalton Jones is one of America's most renowned and celebrated authors, and his latest, *The Problem of Life,* is one of his most successful and important works, bringing resolution to the life and times of his most treasured tragic protagonist."

PART I

One

It was 4:33 A.M., Dalton Jones sat on the edge of his bed in the dark listening to the December wind rattle the glass panes of his bedroom windows. He took a couple of deep breaths. He was tired, but couldn't sleep—his body ached. When he stood up, the old cat jumped off the other side of the bed and disappeared down the upstairs hall. Dalton stood there for a moment in his bedroom, then walked slowly to the bathroom. He turned on the light and sat on the toilet. The old cat, Sam, followed him and rubbed against the calf of his leg.

Dalton drew a hot bath, and as the bathtub filled with water, Sam moved across the room and hopped up onto the wooden stool next to the tub. Dalton stood at the sink looking in the mirror at his weathered face and body, wondering what happened to his life, then cleared his sinuses and spit in the sink.

When the tub was full, Dalton lowered himself down into the hot water. It burned and momentarily numbed the pain in his lower back. Old age was hell—always something new—like constant maintenance to a sinking ship. Dalton reached over the side of the tub and searched for the fifth of whiskey he'd left there the day before. He found it and removed the plastic cap, took a deep breath, tilted the bottle back filling his mouth with warm whiskey, and swallowed. He sat the bottle on the edge of the tub and sank back down into the hot water.

He had a doctor's appointment this morning—didn't want to go, but knew better than to skip it. He wondered if it snowed last night, and if his truck would start, and thought about what to eat for break-fast, if anything. He opened his eyes and Sam was still sitting on the stool watching the tub's faucet drip hot water. Dalton looked at his old toes, pale skin, and thin white hair on his body, then he noticed the burned out light bulb above the vanity, and the cob webs in the corner of the room. He looked up at the inside of the shower curtain and saw small spots of black mildew and wondered when he last changed it, or scrubbed out the tub for that matter. He took another long drink from the bottle of whiskey, and closed his eyes.

After he took the last swallow of whiskey, he set the empty bottle on the floor next to the tub, and old Sam touched Dalton's arm with his paw—a gentle reminder that he was still there. Dalton drained the water and with effort stood up and got out of the tub. As he toweled off, he looked at himself in the mirror again. "I was young once Sam," he said. "So much for the golden years, this seems more like tarnished brass."

It was dark outside when Dalton made his way downstairs. He still had the dull ache in his back—the whiskey had helped some, but not enough. He walked through the living room to the kitchen. Through the window over the sink he could see it was snowing, and in the distance, past the swaying white pines, he watched a freighter passing over Lake Michigan. Dalton turned on the light above the sink, made coffee, and fed old Sam. He sat at the kitchen table sipping black coffee and listening to the wall clock tick. Once he finished his coffee, he found his gloves and hat, and put on his boots. Sam sat on the counter top watching out the kitchen window as Dalton left the house.

With a broken ice scrapper he cleaned off the windshield, then got into the old Ford truck and slammed the door. He was glad when the truck started up—he didn't want to mess with a dead battery this morning. He turned the defroster on high, shifted into second gear and rolled through the fresh snow down the driveway. He drove in silence along Cathead Bay Road, then winding over the rolling pine covered hills of 629 south into Northport. He drove slowly through town to his doctor's office across the street from the Leelanau Medical Center. He parked the truck across from the entrance, climbed out, and slammed the door. When inside he stomped his feet, knocking the snow off his boots. He started down the hall to his doctor's office, walked in, and up to the counter where a young receptionist was messing with her cell phone—texting or some damn thing. She didn't make eye contact with Dalton until he cleared his throat, then she looked up, seemingly irritated.

"Can I help you?" She asked.

"I've got an appointment to see Dr. Mackenzie," Dalton said.

"You'll need to sign in," she said abruptly, then spun around in the chair and walked out of the front office. Dalton could see where to sign in, but there wasn't a pen.

"Excuse me," he said, "Miss?" She walked back looking even more irritated. "A pen?" She walked over and set a pen on the counter in front of him, then the office phone rang and she turned away to answer it. Dalton thought of a handful of things he'd like to say, but refrained. As he signed his name she hung up the phone and disappeared into the back again, and Dalton went to sit down. Across the waiting room from Dalton was Eugene Wixson, the 87-year-old owner of Grandview, Northport's oldest bar. Eugene had been watching Dalton since he walked in.

"Miserable shit," Eugene said as Dalton sat down.

"Pardon me?" said Dalton with a raised eyebrow.

"I said she's a miserable shit!" Eugene said again. "You losing your hearing Jones?"

"No," Dalton said. "Morning Eugene."

"She's that friendly every time I come here," Eugene said. "These god damn young people don't know how good they have it just to be able to get out of bed in the mornings—not to piss themselves every time they sneeze. Hell, she's so homely, she probably just needs a good lay to bring her out of her misery."

"Think you're the man for the job?" Dalton said as he picked up a magazine.

"By god I could be," Eugene said. He folded the newspaper he was reading and moved over and sat next to Dalton. "What ya in for Jones?"

"Just some routine stuff," Dalton said turning the pages of the magazine.

"What?" Eugene yelled as if he were still across the room. He stuck his finger in his ear adjusting the volume of his hearing aid—it started whistling and he turned it back down. "I need some rest too," Eugene said, "I hate these early appointments." Dalton nodded in agreement, continuing to turn the pages of the magazine, not feeling much like socializing.

"I picked up that new book of yours everyone's talking about," Eugene said.

"Oh yeah?" Dalton said, mildly interested.

"Read some of it—not my thing. I like westerns. Louis L'Amour. Now there was a writer. Ever read any of that?"

"Yep," Dalton said, "a whole bunch of it."

"Ever wrote a western?" Eugene asked, but before Dalton had a chance to answer Eugene continued, "hasn't been a good western movie in years—not since John Wayne died." Dalton wasn't sure where the conversation was going. "You know, you look more like your old man everyday," Eugene said. "You know I used to work with him in the cannery back in… oh hell it was a long time ago. Knew your cousin Edward too—I still think of him every once in a while. I knew him pretty well. You moved away before I got to know you—but I know you now!"

"Yes you do," Dalton said, shifting in his chair and closing the magazine.

"Where'd you say you moved to back then?"

"New York," Dalton said, looking out the window watching snow accumulate on the windows ledge.

"That's right," Eugene said, then sat quiet for a moment. "Terrible thing about those towers a few years back—I guess they're rebuilding them even bigger this time. I never had the desire to live in a big city like that. Always been happy out where it's quiet, not a lot of commotion." Eugene paused to cough into a hanker-chief.

"You know I have nine grandchildren, and I haven't seen but one of them since last year."

"Hmm," said Dalton, not really concerned.

"You notice I haven't been around for a few weeks?"

"Can't say I have," Dalton said, but he had.

"Well, you know, last year when I got so sick and that granddaughter of mine, Adley—my god shes a wonderful girl. She came up to help out in the bar. Well, a few weeks ago I went down to Saginaw to stay with her mother—my oldest daughter, Nancy—and she decided it was time to put me in one of them old folks homes. I told her I didn't need that, but she insisted, so I went. I was there for about a week and I called Adley—who was here taking care of the bar. I told her to come and get me. I haven't told Nancy yet… oh she probably knows by now…. It's nice to be back in Northport. Good place to come home to, you know what I mean?"

"Sure do," said Dalton.

A nurse walked out, a middle aged woman with a pretty face.

"Mr. Jones?" she said looking at her clipboard.

"I'm here," Dalton said, the entire lower half of his body ached as he stood up. He turned to Eugene, "I'll see you later."

"See you tonight," Eugene said, unfolding the newspaper he was reading before Dalton walked into the office. Dalton followed the nurse down the hall to Dr. Mackenzie's office, and took a seat close to the window.

"The doctor will be right with you Mr. Jones," the nurse said and left the room.

Dalton shifted in his chair, no position was comfortable this morning. He looked around the office, certificates on the wall, pictures of Mackenzie's family, and his boat. There was a glass fish paperweight on his desk. Dalton looked out the window—it was snowing even harder. The office door swung open and Dr. Aaron Mackenzie walked in.

"Dalton," Aaron said. The two men shook hands.

"Aaron."

Aaron Mackenzie moved around to the back of his desk and sat down.

"We've got all the results back from the PSA tests, and the biopsy, and it's about what I expected. Dalton, every few weeks I have to give someone bad news..." Aaron said as he took off his glasses and rubbed his eyes with his fore finger and thumb.

"Just say it," Dalton said.

Aaron paused for a moment longer.

"The six core samples taken from your prostate during the biopsy determined that you have an aggressive high-grade prostate cancer. It's metastasized to the bone."

"What can you do?" Dalton asked. He was shocked. He'd anticipated this visit to be like all the rest—another close call—then he'd be read the riot act for not exercising, and drinking too much—but not this... not cancer.

"The options are a surgical prostatectomy, bracing therapy, external beam radiation, hormone therapy... this cancer should be treated as aggressively as possible. I'd like to start with the hormones, then a series of daily radiation. The prostate cancer cells feed off the testosterone the body produces, so shutting down the production of testosterone with the hormone therapy can in effect starve the cancer and improve the radiations effectiveness." Aaron put his glasses back on. "This cancer has metastasized to the bone and is reducing your bone density, meaning you're at risk of bone fractures. Dalton, I think treatment should begin soon."

"I... don't know," Dalton said in disbelief. "When?"

"I can arrange it to start as early as this afternoon."

"No... no," said Dalton. "I have to go to New York this weekend to see my son. Next week. Maybe...."

"Alright," Aaron said while writing out a prescription, "But you call me as soon as you get back. Until then I'm going to write you a few prescriptions to help you sleep and for the pain. If there's any more pain than what your experiencing now... Dalton, you call me night or day. I'll drive out to your place if need be."

"Aaron, if I don't do this therapy and radiation, how long…?"

"Hard to say. This cancer is advanced and extremely aggressive. Perhaps a month or two. Maybe three untreated."

"And treated?" Dalton asked.

"It would depend on how your body reacts to the treatment," Aaron said. "It could prolong your life up to a year, or two possibly."

"No cure though?" Dalton asked.

Aaron shook his head. "Not at this stage, I'm sorry."

Dalton understood, and stood up. "Okay… all right," Dalton said in a daze. "I'll call you next week…"

"Are you all right?" Aaron asked. "You want a ride home?"

Dalton shook his head no, "I'll call ya next week."

Two

Dalton pulled out of the parking lot—he wasn't sure how long he'd sat at the stop sign when the car behind him honked their horn. He pulled the truck over to the curb and let the car pass. He sat there in silence as the defroster blew warm air on the windshield and into his eyes. He was trying to remember everything Aaron had said—but all he could remember was the word *cancer*. He wished he'd never left home this morning as he sat there watching snow melt as it hit the windshield. All at once he was flooded with regret—the ones he thought he never had—and wondered what happened to his life. He wished he was younger, some place warmer. He thought about his ex-wife Lilly, and what a lousy father he'd been to his son Dan. All the times he should've been there for them, and wasn't—all the things he wished he would've said to them. He wished he would've written more, or bought that place in Key West, Florida. He wished he hadn't let all that time slip away. Now it was too late. For the first time in years, he felt scared.

Dalton drove south to a small diner in Peshawbestown. He sat in a booth next to a steamed up window and drank black coffee. The waitress, a young girl, looked tired and didn't speak besides asking him if he wanted more coffee. He sat there for a long time trying to think of what it was one should be thinking about when told they're going to die. All his previous thoughts and plans were wiped away, and he was searching for a place to begin in preparation for the end. He wondered what does he do now? He wondered if he should tell his family? He finished his cup of coffee, put some money on the table, and left the diner. He wiped the snow off his windshield and when he started up the old truck, the defroster was still blowing on high. Dalton drove slowly back into Northport.

He pulled up to a stop sign and noticed Angela Bartlett walking along the snow covered sidewalk. Seeing her broke his train of thought, like coming up for air. He pulled up next to her, leaned over and swung the passenger door open.

"Angie," he yelled to get her attention, "get in." Angie looked startled standing there as snow accumulated on her wet hair and jacket. She smiled and climbed into the truck.

"Slam it hard or you'll get a draft," Dalton said, and she slammed the door. "Car broke down again?"

"Yeah," said Angie.

Dalton stepped on the clutch, shifted the truck into gear, and rolled on through town.

"How'd Billy get to school?" Dalton asked.

"He walked. Didn't have much of a choice."

"You should've called," Dalton said. They went a few blocks in silence while she rubbed her hands together trying to warm them. "Where's mister what's-his-name?"

"Paul?" Angie said.

"Yeah—the guy I met a few months back."

"We broke up," Angie said. "He moved out a few days ago."

"Oh," Dalton said as he turned the corner onto Nagonaba Street, and pulled up in front of Tom's Food Market.

"I'll be by tonight, pick you up and take a look at your car."

"Oh Dalton, you don't have to."

"I insist—it's too damn cold to be walking all over. Besides you don't even have a warm jacket—you're going to catch pneumonia."

"Thanks Dalton," she said.

He nodded.

"I'll see you tonight," he said. Angie smiled, climbed out, and slammed the door shut. Dalton watched her go into the store; she sure was a pretty little thing he thought, and he hated seeing her in the position she was in. She was proud and wanted to do it all on her own—but this car stuff—Dalton knew she didn't know a damn thing about cars, and he insisted on helping out when he could. Besides, it would take his mind off things.

He pulled around the corner still thinking about Angie, and there on the sidewalk was his brother-in-law, Charlie Stevens, zipping up his coat. Next to him was his Australian shepherd, Hank Williams. When Charlie saw Dalton he waved with both hands above his head, and Hank barked. Dalton rolled down his window as he came to a stop.

"You lost?" Dalton said.

"Have been for years," Charlie said. "Going my way?" Charlie lived about a mile out of town, and hardly ever drove his car.

"Hop in," said Dalton.

Charlie and Hank hurried around the truck and climbed in. Hank was in the middle, and Charlie slammed the door as Dalton shifted the truck into gear and rolled out of town.

"Cold this morning," Charlie said, and coughed a little. "By god I got a tickle in my throat I just can't shake," Charlie said rubbing his throat.

"It's in the glove box," Dalton said. Charlie grinned, opened the glove box and pulled out a pint of whiskey. He removed the cap and took a drink, offered it to Dalton, but he shook his head. Dalton considered telling Charlie about his appointment, and news, and then decided against it—not yet.

Charlie Stevens married Dalton's older sister Meg and was probably the dearest friend Dalton ever had, next to his cousin Edward. Dalton and Charlie had seen a lot of life together over the years. Dalton loved his sister Meg too. She was the mothering type, always moving around and never happy unless she was feeding or nurturing someone. He thought she'd have been a great mother had she been able to have kids. Dalton always thought what irony it was that he was able to have a child and did such a lousy job with parenthood. When he'd make those types of comments around Meg, she'd say, "Now Dalton, you did what you know, you were no different than Daddy was with us kids. You did the best you could." Dalton appreciated her kindness, but knew it wasn't true.

"So what are you doing in town so early?" Charlie asked.

"Gave Angie Bartlett a ride into work," Dalton said.

"Car trouble?"

Dalton nodded yes.

"You tell her you're going to New York to see Dan?"

"Didn't come up," Dalton said.

"You ever offer any information about Dan?"

"Nope." Dalton shifted into third as the old truck rolled around the corner. He held out his hand and Charlie passed him the bottle. Dalton took a drink and handed it back to Charlie, who took another drink.

"She ever talk to you about that boy of hers?" Charlie asked.

Dalton shot him a dirty look. He pushed in the clutch and shifted into neutral as he turned the wheel, steering the truck into Charlie's unplowed driveway. When Dalton came to a stop, Hank got impatient and barked—Charlie swung open his door and Hank dove out of the cab.

"You better come in or your sister will be upset," Charlie said passing the bottle back to Dalton. He took the last swallow and stuck the empty bottle back in the glove box. Dalton and Charlie walked up to the house where Hank sat anxiously by the side door. When they walked inside, Meg stepped out of the pantry and thought the boys looked mischievous, like children. Hank barked before he crawled under the kitchen table, and Meg touched Dalton on the arm and said good morning.

"You boys hungry?" Meg asked as she put her apron on and started a fresh pot of coffee. She didn't need a response. She prepared a meal at lightening speed—Meg was selfless, and amazing. She moved around the kitchen as if it were a perfectly choreographed dance, all the while Charlie was saying things to her like, "Your looking lovely this morning dear. Did you do something different with your hair?" and "Have I told you how much I love you today?" and Meg would giggle like a schoolgirl and carry on. When they embraced their bellies rubbed together, and they still seemed in love after so many years. Dalton had always been in awe of their relationship.

Meg served fried eggs, sausage and toast, and poured them each another hot cup of coffee. She washed a few dishes, then sat down at the table with a cup of coffee and her recipe book—only to jump up again and rush into the other room. Carlie and Dalton continued to eat, and she came back shortly.

"I almost forgot," Meg said, "Look whose in the paper this morning!" She handed the folded newspaper to Dalton, pointing at the article… "Elizabeth! Can you believe it! She's going to be lecturing at the university this Friday. We should all go and say hello!"

Dalton swallowed hard when he saw the headline and the photo of Elizabeth Wharton. He stared at the newspaper and didn't say a word. Seeing her image there in the paper and hearing her name—his heart fluttered and ached.

"When was the last time you saw Elizabeth?" Meg asked.

Dalton took a deep breath and could feel the ache in his back and groin return.

"Oh, … I don't know Meg," Dalton said—but he did know, he remembered every moment. "It's been a few years."

"We should go and listen to her speak and say hello," Meg said as she sat back down at the table looking at the picture of Elizabeth in the paper. "That would be so nice, what do you think Charlie? Will you go?"

Charlie, who was drinking his coffee, shrugged.

Meg handed the paper back across the table to Dalton, and he folded it and set it aside. "We really should go, it's been so long—and we were all such good friends." She started to get a little choked up and misty eyed. "It seems like a life time ago doesn't it?"

"Maybe Meg," Dalton said, and sipped his coffee. He wanted to change the subject. "I don't have a lot of time."

"That's all we do have!" Meg laughed. "I'd just love to see her again. I've always felt bad that we drifted apart after Edward died,"

Meg said quickly wiping away a tear. Charlie looked over at Dalton, who was now staring down into his empty coffee cup. "What do you say Charlie" Meg persisted, "will you go?"

Unlike Meg, Charlie knew what had come between Elizabeth and Dalton.

"Meg, darling, did we finish off that apple pie?" Charlie asked, knowing they hadn't. "That would sure go good with this coffee," Charlie said with a smile. His request distracted Meg, who jumped up and cut a piece of pie for the men and warmed up their coffee.

There wasn't a lot of conversation as they finished their pie. Then Dalton excused himself, kissed Meg on top of the head and started for the door. Hank was out from under the table and Dalton stepped over him. As he put on his coat, Meg got up and handed him the folded newspaper.

"Think about going to see Elizabeth—if Charlie will take me, I'd like to go. If you have time, maybe you could come with us," Meg said. Dalton forced a slight smile while glancing over at Charlie, who said nothing. Dalton told Meg he'd think about it, thanked her for breakfast and left.

When Dalton got home, he got out of the truck and left the folded newspaper on the front seat. He walked around the house out to the shoreline of Cathead Bay. As he approached the water, he could hear the waves and the rustling of the few leaves that clung to winter's trees. The air was cold. The water was low and the exposed rocks along the shore seemed vulnerable. Dalton stared across the bay to Lake Michigan, to the horizon where the water and grey sky met. He felt like he was at the end of the Earth out here on the peninsula. He loved the solitude, loathed the loneliness. He pushed his hands into his jacket pockets and thought about his life here in Northport, his parents, his sister and cousin Edward. He thought about having cancer, and what this was going to do to him. He wondered how bad the pain would get—and how Meg would handle all this when the time came to tell her. Then he thought about that folded newspaper and Elizabeth Wharton. Seeing her picture, hearing her name, took him back in time.

A long time ago Dalton had dreamed of accomplishing so much more, and thought he would have made such a difference in the world—that he would've done it through his writing. As he grew older he realized his writing wasn't for the world, it was for him. It allowed him to look inside, to grow, and to deal with emotions he felt but never spoke of. Writing had been his life, and his written words were the footprints he'd leave behind.

What had Dalton learned after all these years, experiences, and words? What meaning could be drawn from this life? At one point he would have said it was all about family, but not today. His wife, Lilly, left him and was living her life out with another man. His son Dan was distant... and Dalton wondered if that relationship would even exist if the monthly allowance stopped. He loved Dan, and understood he had many of the same dreams Dalton had as a young man, but Dalton never had a father paying all the bills—he had to struggle for everything in life. Dalton wondered if he'd made life too easy for Dan. He questioned himself, isn't it the struggle and journey through life that builds character and makes one a man? For a while, Dalton felt the money he sent Dan was a good substitute for love in a long distance relationship. Money also was an easy fix after years of neglect. But now, facing cancer and perhaps the end of his life—Dalton realized that there was no substitute for the time he should have spent with his son.

Three

Above the chaos of Midtown Manhattan, Dan Jones sat in the quiet office of his agent, Monica Galiano, waiting to hear the response of the publisher who'd just reviewed his latest novel. He was sweating, and tried to relax as Monica hung up the phone.

"Well?" Dan asked.

Monica smiled hesitantly.

"They're interested in you—just not this novel," Monica said. "They said they really needed something big. Now don't take this wrong… but they suggested a book about your father—just think, you could be the first to write an authorized biography on him—now that would be big—sure to get their attention." Monica leaned forward on the desk. "Their just not interested in new fiction right now."

Dan tried to keep a straight face and to not show his defeat. Monica stood up and went to her filing cabinet, opened the top drawer and pulled out a large manila envelope. Leaning across her desk, she handed it to Dan. It was the copy of the novel he'd submitted… "They had a courier deliver this earlier this morning," she said.

Dan took it from her. "You know, it's not the end of the world. We'll keep submitting it, and in the mean time, why don't you give them what they want—it'd be a foot in the door," Monica said.

"I don't know. I'm not sure how my father would even feel about it," Dan said. "I just wanted to do something without mentioning his name for once." Dan knew that his biggest problem was that he was accustom to doors opening quickly—people admired his father, and a lot of things came easy for Dan because of it.

Resolving Dalton Jones

Dan thanked Monica, left her office, and caught the 6 train downtown. As he walked down Saint Marks Place it started to rain and he flipped his jacket collar up and shoved his hands deep into his pockets. The manila envelope tucked under his arm was getting wet, but he didn't care. He made his way down the block to the *Grassroots Tavern*, down the steps, and pushed open the door. Inside, it was warm and smelled of old wood. A cat made its way down the bar, weaving it's way around beer bottles. The bartender, a quiet man of about sixty, was closing the till. The old wooden floors creaked as Dan made his way to the dim lit bar, and music played on the jukebox. He thought how this place had the same feel as the Grandview, the old bar back in Northport, and how his father would like it here. Dan placed the damp envelope on the bar and sat on a bar stool. The quiet bartender stepped up, didn't say anything, just made eye contact. He knew who Dan was—he'd seen hundreds like him over the years. Dan ordered a whiskey and Coke, "Heavy on the whiskey," he said—he didn't even need to say that—the quiet bartender already knew what Dan was looking for. He prepared the drink, set it in front of him, and walked away. Dan took a long drink, and then looked at the envelope with the rejected novel inside. He'd worked so hard on it—and was sure this was going to be the one. He'd been writing for the last three years, one story after another, and nothing ever came of any of them—but he thought this one was different. Obviously it wasn't. Maybe he wasn't supposed to be a writer, maybe he should've given up a long time ago. He looked down into his drink and thought about Julie, his girlfriend and roommate for the last seven months. He knew he'd hung on to her too long too, and needed to let her go. He finished his drink and ordered another. The first time he met Julie he fell for her. She became everything to him. He ignored her flaws and bad habits and put her on a pedestal, but now after seven months together in a small apartment the novelty was gone.

An old Johnny Cash song started to play on the jukebox— Dan liked this song, this drink, this bar stool. It was all he needed tonight. He wondered where the hell was he going from here?

All he'd thought about for so long was this damn novel—it'd become his life—and this rejection hurt bad.

The last time he talked to his father he bragged that his agent was working on getting it published. Dalton seemed happy for Dan, and proud of him. Dalton could relate to Dan for what seemed the ·first time, and it was a validation for Dan—the respect of his father meant everything. Dalton had just published yet another novel, getting great reviews—and now Dan's was rejected. When Dalton was Dan's age he'd already published three novels and numerous short stories. Dan wondered what he'd say when Dalton asked about the novel. He felt like his life had been a series of failures up to this point, and if not for Dalton's monthly checks, Dan couldn't even afford his rent. He ordered another drink and hung onto the bar. His cell phone rang and he fished it out of his pocket—it was Julie. He thought about answering it, then decided against it. He didn't want to talk to her—to have to pretend to be interested in what she had to say. He just wanted to be alone for a while. He shut off the phone and took another drink.

Four

Around 5:30 P.M. Dalton pulled the old Ford up in front of Tom's Food Market. Angie ran out and climbed inside. They made small talk about the weather and people they knew as he drove her home. When they got to her place—a little house she had rented for years—Dalton parked out front on the street. As they climbed out of the truck and walked over to Angie's car, Dalton could see Angie's mother and son Billy through the front window.

"Got the keys?" Dalton asked.

Angie pulled the keys out of her pocket and dangled them in the air.

"Pop the hood," Dalton said, "and try to turn it over." As Dalton propped open the hood, he could see Angie's little boy Billy smiling from the window, and Angie's mother was looking out through the screen door—she didn't smile, just stood there with a dirty look on her face. Angie tried to start the car, but nothing happened.

"It's not doing anything," she said.

"It's your battery," said Dalton. "When did you change it last?"

"I don't even know," Angie said.

Dalton shook his head and shut the hood.

"Well, I'll pick up another battery tomorrow and we'll get her running."

"I appreciate your help Dalton," Angie said.

"It ain't no big deal. It's the least I could do."

"You know, you don't owe me anything," Angie said.

"God damn it Angie," Dalton said, "Ain't that what friends do?"

Angie was taken back by his tone, but then she smiled.

"You wanna come in for a cup of coffee?" She asked.

Dalton looked over to the house where Angie's mother stood scowling.

"No. I better go," he said, and made his way back to the pickup. Angie waved goodbye and smiled as he drove away. She never figured Dalton thought of her as a friend, but she was glad he did. When she went into the house her mother said, "You look out for him! He's a dirty old man!"

"Oh Mother," Angie laughed.

Five

Charlie Stevens turned the corner and continued walking down Waukazoo Street. Hank was at his side. He saw Dalton's truck parked out front of the Grandview and noticed the falling snow hadn't accumulated on the hood. Charlie went inside and stomped his feet and Hank followed him in.

"Evening Charles," Eugene said, then took a long drag off a cigarette. Dalton was in his usual place in back writing in his journal. He glanced up and saw Charlie, and then went back to writing. Charlie took off his hat and gloves and sat down at the bar. Hank sat at his feet.

"How bout a cold beer and a shot of whiskey to warm me up," Charlie said unwrapping his scarf. As Eugene poured Charlie a double, ashes from his cigarette fell on the bar. He put the whiskey in front of Charlie, then a cold can of Budweiser.

"What's new?" Eugene asked, sitting down on his stool behind the bar.

"Besides this cold, not a god damn thing," Charlie said.

"How's Meg?" asked Eugene as Charlie sipped his whiskey.

"She's fine, she's fine. All locked away from the cold with the furnace turned up. Says she loves this time of the year—but never leaves the house."

Eugene smiled and ashed his cigarette.

In the back, Dalton finished writing, closed his journal, and went up to the bar to sit with Charlie.

"Not much to say today?" Charlie said to Dalton, referring to his writing.

Dalton shook his head.

"Eugene, I'll have another," Dalton said. Eugene poured whiskey into his glass.

"Been here long?" Charlie asked.

"Not long," Dalton said. They both watched the weather forecast on the little TV behind the bar. Eugene turned the volume up and lit another cigarette.

"Anything exciting happen since I saw you last?" Charlie asked.

"Hell, I just saw you this morning," Dalton said. They both took a drink.

"Sorry about that whole newspaper thing this morning, Meg was so excited..."

"It doesn't matter," Dalton interrupted. "She means well."

"Hear that boys!" Eugene said, pointing to the TV, "More snow tonight! Jesus Christ, it's never going to end. So much for global warming!" Eugene got up from his stool and went to the back room behind the bar. Dalton turned and watched the falling snow through the big window out front. It was getting dark outside and the snow was sticking to the roads and rooftops. Icy wind blew across the Leelanau Peninsula, and he imagined the children in Northport were praying for a snow-day and no school tomorrow, while mothers prepared meals, and fathers pulled out the snow blowers and snow shovels, all while watching the evening sky that smelled of wood burning stoves and fireplaces. Dalton could see down the street to the Filling Station, where a fat old man was setting up a donation box for the Salvation Army, and then smoked a cigarette. A big truck passed. It was the Shurburne's bringing in a truck load of Christmas trees from Meesick—the sweet smell of fresh cut pine in December—short, fat, tall trees, all to be bought and decorated for the holidays.

Fred Anderson walked in, waved to Dalton and Charlie, and then set down at the other end of the bar. Fred was the owner and director of the only funeral home in town since the late sixties, and he knew everyone.

Eugene walked down to the other end of the bar and started talking politics with Fred. Charlie, still sitting next to Dalton, was in a perfectly relaxed state—thanks to the warm bar and whiskey.

"Does the hardware store still have those car batteries on sale?" Dalton asked.

"Yeah," Charlie said. "Truck giving you problems?"

"No. I'm going to pick one up for Angie Bartlett in the morning."

Charlie paused and looked over at Dalton. "Can I ask you something?" said Charlie.

Dalton clenched his jaw, he had a good idea where this was going.

"I don't ever pry into your affairs, you know that, and you don't even got to answer if you don't want to, but I gotta ask…"

"Well?" Dalton said, growing impatient.

"Is that boy of hers your grandson?"

"Goddammit Charlie—you've asked me that question a hundred times!" Dalton growled, frustrated, squirming on his bar stool. "How the hell would I know? I don't know—*Jesus Christ*!"

"Wouldn't you rather me ask than go around wondering, not saying anything?"

"I don't know," Dalton repeated. "It's not my business!"

"You know that's what people say," said Charlie.

"*Goddammit*, Charlie—what people?" Eugene headed back towards them as Dalton downed his drink.

"You boys talking politics too?" said Eugene.

"How about another round for me and my brother-in-law," Charlie said. Eugene reached for the whiskey and poured as Dalton stared hard out the window. Charlie went back to watching the local news on the small TV. When Eugene finished pouring, Dalton and Charlie simultaneously took a drink.

"I had a doctor's appointment this morning—that's why I was in town," Dalton said.

"You sick?" Charlie asked. There was a long pause.

"I got cancer," Dalton said. Charlie sat real still, staring towards the television. Then he turned to look at Dalton. "Prostate cancer, it's spread—it's pretty bad."

"What can they do?" Charlie said in almost a whisper.

"Mackenzie wants to do radiation and start some therapy—but he said at this stage it would probably only prolong it."

Charlie sat in silent anguish, nodded, and took another drink.

"How are you feeling?"

"Like hell most of the time. I ache, I'm tired, I haven't been myself. That's why I went to the doctor in the first place. Hell, I just thought it was old age. Mackenzie gave me a hard time for not coming in sooner."

They both sat there for a long moment.

"You haven't told Meg yet have you?" Charlie asked.

"Not yet," Dalton said, "I will."

"What about Dan?"

"No."

"You still planning on the trip to New York?" Charlie asked.

"Yes," Dalton said.

Charlie nodded.

"You know, I didn't mean to upset you with that question earlier," Charlie said.

"I know you didn't."

"You know I love you like my own brother," said Charlie.

"I know." Dalton said.

The two men sat together for a long time that night staring at the little television behind the bar. They didn't talk much—they didn't have too.

Six

At 4:27 A.M. Dalton opened his eyes. He lay there in the dark a while before he got up. Old Sam was still asleep on the other side of the bed. Dalton took a couple of deep breaths—he ached way down deep inside. He put on a flannel shirt, jeans and warm socks, and went downstairs.

He walked into the kitchen, past the folded newspaper on the table, turned on the light and made a pot of coffee. He noticed the answering machine was blinking and he played the message…

"Dalton—Jonathan price. I've went ahead and made all the arrangements for the book signing in Traverse City in a few weeks. I just wanted to touch base with you. Great review in the New York Times. *Well, call me when you get a moment."*

Dalton walked back to the table, picked up the newspaper and read the article about Elizabeth Wharton. It said she was giving a lecture tomorrow night on her career, as part of the Modern Women lecture series at the Northwestern Michigan College in Traverse City. According to the article Elizabeth was a resident of Midland Michigan, and taught painting and drawing at Central Michigan University.

He tossed the paper back on the table, then got his journal out of his bag and sat down to write. Steam came out the front of the coffee maker as hot water trickled down into the pot. Sam rubbed up against the calf of Dalton's leg, then jumped up on the table and stretched while flexing his front paws.

It was still dark outside. Dalton could see his reflection in the big picture window, and could hear the cold wind howl as it blew around the house. He opened his journal and wrote the date at the top left of the page, then the time, 4:49 A.M. He wrote about the day before, starting with his appointment, and then on through the evening at the Grandview with Charlie. He wrote about all the things he kept inside and wasn't able to share. He'd saved thousands of dollars in therapy sessions over the years by being able to write it all out.

Years ago, after his ex-wife, Lilly, divorced him, he was depressed and locked himself away here in the house. He was drinking heavy and wouldn't talk to anyone. His sister Meg finally got through to him and asked him to see a therapist.

At first he said no, but when she cried, he agreed to it. She made his first appointment, and even drove him. The therapist was a young woman—half of Dalton's age. She sat across the office from him behind a big desk, and he sat at the other end on a giant couch. The woman started out asking him vague questions about childhood and his parents. Dalton answered her questions while she sat at her desk writing as fast as she could. She would pause, glance at her watch, and then go back to asking vague questions. The fourth time she looked at her watch, Dalton asked her if she had someplace to be, "I beg your pardon?" she replied.

"You've looked at your watch four times in the last ten minutes," Dalton said.

"Oh," she said. "I'm keeping track of our session."

"Are you ever going to ask me why I'm here?" Dalton asked. She only stared back at him from across the room. "I'm sorry Ma'am— I don't think you and I are going to get much accomplished here. Besides that, you look like your younger than my kid, and I don't see how any advice from you is going to help me much."

Dalton walked out of the office leaving the young woman sitting speechless and alone at her big desk.

A few weeks later Meg talked him into seeing a different therapist. She said they're like boots—you have to try a few on before you settle on a pair. To make her happy, he agreed to it one last time. This time he drove himself to the appointment. The office was about the same as the last one, but this guy's desk wasn't so far away. The therapist was a man in his late forties or early fifties. The appointment started out fine; they talked casually, he explained that he wanted Dalton to feel at ease, and that everything they talked about was strictly confidential. By the end of the first session—which Dalton felt went all right—the therapist wrote a prescription out for a mild anti-depressant and told Dalton he believed that he was suffering from severe depression and was attempting to self medicate with alcohol. He wanted Dalton to start off with this mild drug, and they could increase the dosage if needed. Then he pulled out his schedule and wanted to set up appointments with Dalton for the next six months. Dalton went from feeling slightly comfortable to feeling like this guy was trying to sell him a lame horse. He tensed up and clenched his teeth. He looked at the prescription the guy had handed him, and threw it back on the desk.

Dalton stood up. "You've known me less than an hour, and you think you have me all figured out—writing prescriptions and ready for me to join up with the year membership!" he said.

"Mr. Jones—please, sit down, I want to help you…"

"You want to help me? Why don't we go down the street and get a drink, and talk—and you can get out from behind that expensive desk of yours!"

"Mr. Jones, I can't…"

"I bet you can't. I'm sorry we've wasted one another's time," Dalton said and walked out, slamming the door.

He drove back to Northport and parked the truck out front of the Grandview, Eugene waved as Dalton walked inside.

"Afternoon Jones—ain't seen you in a while."

Dalton nodded, and mumbled something about whiskey and went to the back of the bar and sat down with a new journal notebook and started to write.

That evening when Charlie went home, he told Meg that whatever she'd been saying to Dalton must have worked because he was back at the Grandview that evening writing like crazy.

Meg was in her chair crocheting an afghan, she looked up over her glasses and smiled. Regardless of how the appointment went, she was glad Dalton was out of the house and writing again. It had taken him several months, a case and a half of whiskey, and two therapists to realize something he and Meg already knew—he was more comfortable writing about his feeling than talking about them.

To Dalton, that all seemed like such a long time ago now. He finished his coffee and stepped over to the counter and poured whiskey into his empty coffee cup, then sat back down and continued to write for the next couple hours. He wrote about everything except what was foremost on his mind, and that was Elizabeth Wharton. Between every sentence, there she was, resurfacing. Several times he started to write something about her, but he just held the pen above the paper—no words came, only a dull sadness that ached as if an old wound had been reopened.

When Dalton was finished writing, he went upstairs and took a hot shower. Sam sat on the wooden stool next to the tub. Afterwords, Dalton got dressed in another flannel shirt, jeans, and warm socks. He went down stairs and put on his boots and gloves, and said, "See ya later," to Sam, who was sitting on the corner of the kitchen table. Dalton went outside and cleaned the snow and ice off the windshield of the pickup while it warmed up. It took almost twenty minutes before it started to kick out any heat, but Dalton didn't care. The truck still ran good—and was paid for.

He drove into town to the Ace Hardware on North Mill Street—they had just opened up. He went in and bought a car battery. The sale on them had been over for two days, but the kid running the till sold it to Dalton at the sale price. Dalton loaded the battery into the truck and headed towards Angie's place. He drove past a big yellow school bus with its side windows all iced up, and a lady in an old rusted Chevrolet drove slowly down the street throwing rolled up newspapers onto morning sidewalks. Dalton pulled the truck around the corner onto Angie's street. He saw another car in her driveway, and Angie was standing in the front doorway of the little house, talking to some guy. As Dalton rolled slowly up the unplowed street he realized the guy on the front porch was Paul—the one Angie broke up with a few days before. The closer Dalton got he could see they were arguing. Paul was trying to push his way into the house—then he slapped Angie hard across the face. "Oh, god damn it!" Dalton said out loud. Meaning to step on the brake, he hit the gas instead, and the old Ford bumped over the frozen curb and slid into Angie's front yard. Paul let go of Angie's arm and spun around as Dalton got out of the truck. Dalton looked as mean as an old bull as he made his way across the front yard and up the porch steps.

"Hey old man!" Paul said, holding his hands out as if it would stop Dalton, who walked up to Paul, grabbed him by the front of his jacket, and threw him off the front porch—face first into the snow.

"Dalton!" Angie cried as he climbed back down the steps and walked around to Paul, who was picking himself up. Dalton punched Paul right in the nose, and when Paul fell back into the snow, blood started trickling down his lip and chin.

"My god, you old bastard—you broke my nose!" Paul said.

Dalton stood over him, fists clenched. "You get the hell out of here, you miserable son-of-a-bitch!"

"You *crazy mother fucker!*" Paul yelled. By now some of the neighbors were awake, looking out their front windows, and in the doorway of the house Billy was hanging onto Angie. Paul got up again, ran to his car, and then drove off quickly—slipping and sliding down the street.

Dalton took a deep breath as he stepped back and sat down on the front porch steps. Angie went to his side, "Are you all right?"

"I'm fine," Dalton said breathing heavy, "just old." Angie helped him to his feet and they went inside.

"I'm sorry you got involved Dalton," Angie said. Her face was still red from where Paul hit her.

"What the hell was I suppose to do—watch from the road?" Dalton said.

Billy was across the room, crying and wiping snot from his nose, "He deserved it Mr. Jones," he said.

There was an awkward silence. "What are you doing here anyway?" she asked.

"I got the battery for your car. I was gonna see if we could get it started."

Angie sat down across from him, "Oh Dalton," she sighed. "I'm running late for work, we were just getting ready to leave when…."

"Walking?" Dalton asked. She said yes. Billy coughed and wiped his nose. "I'll drive you." Dalton said, then turned and looked out the window, "If I can get the truck out of your front yard." He groaned as he stood up, he knew he was in no condition to do what he had just done.

Angie didn't want to say it in front of Billy, but she was grateful for what Dalton had done. This wasn't the first time Paul had hit her, but she had a good idea that it was probably the last. Angie hadn't had much luck over the years with men, and wondered why everyone she'd had a relationship with turned out to be rotten. She watched Dalton make his way through the snow to the truck, and wondered if she'd ever find a man like him—if there were even such a thing anymore.

Seven

Dalton dropped Billy off in front of the elementary school on Wing Street, and then he drove Angie to the Leelanau Chamber of Commerce office, south of Suttons Bay on Hilltop Road. She worked there every Tuesday and Thursday answering the phone and emails. This time of year it was slow, but when summer comes the job would increase to full-time again and she'd cut her hours back at Tom's Food Market.

"Dalton, I'm sorry about what happened this morning," Angie said. "I thought everything was going so well with Paul and I, then it seemed like overnight everything changed…"

"You don't have to explain anything to me," Dalton said.

"I know," Angie said. "I guess I'm a little embarrassed by it all. I always thought at this point in my life I'd be settled down somewhere with a good man, and a couple kids. I never dreamed I'd still be here…"

"Why are you?" Dalton asked.

"I don't know. I guess after Billy was born, it was nice being close to my Mom. I didn't have a lot of money. Or education. It would've been hard to leave."

"Nothing worth having is easy," Dalton said.

"I know. Guess I've had this fantasy that someone will come along that loves Billy and I and…."

"You don't need a man to solve your problems, or anyone for that matter."

"I know," Angie said. "It's tough being a single parent.

Overwhelming at times, and it's all I can do to just get through some days."

"You still working on your photography?" Dalton asked.

"Here and there. It's a matter of finding time to do it—it seems pretty low on the priority list most days. How did you find time to write so much over the years?"

"Lilly took care of Dan, and I made writing a priority. I completely neglected them both—you see how well that all worked out for me."

"I guess there must be a balance somewhere," Angie said.

"Between the two of us, your way is better. Billy's the most important thing. I wasn't a very good father or husband." Dalton turned down the defroster and pulled up in front of the Chamber of Commerce's office.

"How much was that battery?" Angie asked.

"Not much, don't worry about it," Dalton said. Angie wanted to protest, but knew it wouldn't make a difference. "I'll come back tonight and pick you up, but first I'm gonna head back over to your place and put this battery in."

"You don't have to do that right now, why don't you wait till later," Angie said.

"What for?" said Dalton. "Don't worry about it, I want to," Dalton said.

"Alright," Angie smiled. She started to get out of the truck. "Oh, you'll need these—the keys to the car, and to the house, if you need to get inside for any reason," Angie said. Dalton took them and stuck them in his pocket.

"Dalton, I want you to know how much I appreciate everything you do for Billy and me."

"You better go to work, young lady," Dalton said changing the subject. She smiled, and climbed out of the truck. Dalton watched her walk carefully over the ice to the front door. Angie turned and waved before she went inside. She was so beautiful, he thought. His son had been a fool for walking away from her the way he did.

Eight

After Dalton put the battery in Angie's car he climbed into the driver's seat, pumped the gas pedal a few times, and turned the ignition—the engine sputtered, then started right up. Dalton was in a lot of pain, so he just sat there and let the car run for a few minutes. He looked up and noticed the gray sky, it looked like more snow was on the way.

When he started for home, he stopped at the Food Market for more whiskey. He figured he'd fill those prescriptions Aaron wrote him tomorrow. Once he got home, Sam was sitting on the kitchen table waiting for him. With some effort, Dalton bent over and took off his boots. Sam followed him up stairs, and when Dalton took a hot bath, Sam patiently sat on the wooden stool next to the tub. After the bath, Dalton went back downstairs and fell asleep in his chair while listening to the morning weather report on the radio. Several hours passed when the telephone rang and woke him up. He got up and walked towards the phone, but waiting for the answering machine to beep.

"*Hello—Dalton, are you there?*" Angie said.

He picked up the phone, "I'm here," he said, "what's happening?"

"Dalton, I hate to ask this of you…" Angie said.

"Yeah, what's going on?" Dalton said.

"The school is closing because of the snow, and I can't find anyone to pick up Billy," She said. "He's coming down with a nasty cold and, would it be too much trouble for you to pick him up?" Angie asked.

"No, no trouble," Dalton said, looking at his coat hanging on the back of the chair.

"The school is closing at noon, but you could pick Billy up anytime," Angie said. "Thank you so much Dalton, Mom is working, and I didn't know who else to call."

"It's no problem," Dalton said. "Is he okay at home alone?"

"Well…" Angie hesitated, "I'm sure he'll be fine for a couple hours."

"How about I bring him out here for the afternoon, then we'll pick you up at 4:00."

"You don't mind?" Angie asked.

"Not at all," Dalton said, looking around the house wondering what the hell he was going to do with a kid all afternoon.

"Oh, thank you, Dalton—if it wasn't so cold I'd just…"

"Angie, it's all right. I'll see you in a while—don't worry about Billy," Dalton said.

They said goodbye and Dalton hung up the phone. He turned and looked out the big window in the kitchen, it was snowing so hard he could bearly see the truck. Sam jumped back on the table, and Dalton took a deep breath. "You ready for some company Sam?" He asked. With some effort he bent over and put his boots back on.

Nine

Dalton walked into the Northport Elementary School. His son, Dan, had attended elementary school in New York, so Dalton had never had a reason to go inside Northport's school. He felt like a giant next to the halls of short lockers and little children roaming around. The office was bustling with activity; teachers talking, phones ringing, students seated along the wall. Dalton felt out of place as he walked up to the counter. He hoped his breath didn't smell like whiskey. He knew the secretary, Betty-Rose Newland. Her husband's company put a new roof on his house about six years earlier. She was a very proper woman—by the book—with tight permed hair, a pressed blouse, and perfectly manicured nails. Her husband had told Dalton one night over beers that she even rolled all the towels up a special way before she put them in the linen closet. Dalton always wanted to see that.

"Good Morning, Betty-Rose," Dalton said.

"May I help you Mr. Jones?" she asked, looking over her bifocals.

"I'm here to pick up William Bartlett."

"Do you have a signed note from one of his parents?"

"What? Oh… no," Dalton said. "His mother, Angie just called and…"

"I'm sorry, we can't release the student without a permission slip signed by the parent."

"God damn it, Betty-Rose," Dalton said.

"Mr. Jones—the children!"

Dalton looked over his shoulder and all the kids in the office were listening attentively. "I don't have a permission slip—can we call his mother or something?" Dalton tried to whisper, but was growing impatient.

Betty-Rose just starred at him while shuffling papers. The phone rang. "Will you excuse me please?" She turned and answered the phone, and started jotting notes down on paper. When she turned back to Dalton, she had another form in her hand.

"Reason for taking the child today?" She asked.

"Isn't the school closing early?" Dalton said.

"Mr. Jones, we still have another thirty minutes before school is out."

"Can you get Billy for me or not?" Dalton asked.

"Normally I would need a signed permission slip from a parent, but…"

"I've known you for twenty years Betty!" Dalton said.

"But!" she said louder, "If you can show me two forms of identification, and sign this release form, I'll let it go today."

"Two forms of ID! Good god, you know who I am!" Dalton said.

"These are difficult times Mr. Jones!"

Dalton grumbled, pulled his wallet out of his back pocket, and put his drivers license and social security card on the counter. Betty-Rose took them and photocopied them, then had Dalton sign the sheet. She had Dalton so worked up at this point he almost forgot how miserable he was feeling.

"Would you like a blood sample too?" Dalton asked as he put his wallet away.

Straight faced, she said, "That won't be necessary," and gave him a dirty look over her bifocals. "Mr. Jones, I'm not sure if you are aware, but our country is at war. Here at Northport elementary we have to be aware of the times—there are terrorists, child molesters, terrible people out there that want to hurt our children, and it is my job to do what I can to keep the children safe. Now please, take a seat and I will call William to the office."

Dalton sat down next to a snotty nosed kid, and when he leaned back in the chair, the kid said, "Excuse me Mister." Dalton looked at him. "Your leaning on the arm of my chair." Dalton looked down at the kid, and the kid just starred back blankly. Dalton shifted to the other side of his chair and said, "That better?" The kid nodded, and wiped the snot from his nose, and went back to starring out the window.

Betty-Rose spoke over the PA, "William Bartlett, William Bartlett, please come to the main office—your ride is here." As she walked back across the office she glared at Dalton again. The following ten minutes he waited for Billy seemed to last an eternity.

Just before the bell rang, Dalton saw Billy coming down the hall. When he stood up and started out the door, Betty-Rose said, "Have a good day Mr. Jones," and gave him a sarcastic smile.

He just grumbled something and left the office. Dalton stood outside the office door as Billy came walking down the hall, and he waved, making sure Billy saw him. Then, the bell rang and it was like a waist high flood wall broke—there were kids everywhere.

"Hi Billy," Dalton said. "Your Mom called and asked if I could pick you up."

"Okay," Billy said. He had his coat and backpack on already.

"Okay," Dalton said, and they went out and got in the truck.

"I figured you could just hang out with me until your mom gets off work," Dalton said.

"Sure," Billy said. Dalton started up the old truck and pulled out of the parking lot. "Aren't you gonna put on your seat belt?" Billy asked.

"What?" said Dalton, "Oh, yeah, I forgot." But he didn't forget, he never wore it—but today he guessed he would.

Ten

It was snowing hard by the time Dalton drove Billy out to the house on Cathead Bay.

"Well, here we are," said Dalton. They climbed out of the truck and went inside.

"You live out here all alone?" Billy asked.

"Yep," Dalton said. "Well, me and old Sam," Dalton said and pointed to the cat sitting on the edge of the kitchen table. The phone rang as Dalton and Billy both took off their coats and hung them on the back of a chair. The phone rang a second and third time.

"You going to answer the phone?" Billy asked. Dalton didn't say anything and waited for the answering machine to pick it up. It was Meg… *"Dalton, are you there?"* He picked up the phone.

"I'm here," he said.

"Betty-Rose called and said you picked Billy up from school. Is everything all right?"

"Good god, she didn't waste any time calling you," Dalton said. "Angie's at work without a car, and I'm just helping out."

"What are you doing for lunch?" Meg asked.

"I don't know—figured we might go back into town, to the Grandview for a burger or something."

"You can't take that child into a bar!" Meg said. "I'll bring over lunch."

"It's snowing like hell!" Dalton said looking out the window.

"You better watch what you say, he's bound to pick those words up from you."

Dalton glanced over to Billy who was petting Sam.

"Oh yeah," Dalton said. "Well, lunch would be great."

"I'll be over in a half an hour—do you want soup, sandwiches, or both?"

"I don't know Meg," Dalton started to get irritated. In a whisper he asked, "What the hell do kids eat?"

"I'll bring both, I'll see you in a minute."

Billy walked into the living room. Dalton hung up the phone and followed behind him.

"How come you don't have any furniture?" Billy asked.

"My wife took it," Dalton said.

"How come?" Billy asked.

"She moved to New York," Dalton said.

"Why did she move there?" Billy asked.

"We used to live there a long time ago. I guess she liked it better."

"Why didn't you go with her?" Billy asked.

"Wasn't invited—you want something to drink?" Dalton asked. Billy nodded, and sat down on the couch. It was one of four pieces of furniture in the big room—a couch, a recliner, an end table with the radio on it, and a small television on a stand.

Dalton went to the kitchen and opened the refrigerator, there were a couple of cans of beer, some eggs, and tomato juice. He looked at the counter top—there was some whiskey and coffee. He poured Billy some tomato juice into a small glass, and when Billy took a drink his face wrinkled up, "What's this?"

"Tomato juice—you don't like it?" Billy shook his head and handed the glass back to Dalton. "How about water?"

"Sure," Billy said.

Soon they were both sitting in the living room watching it snow outside. Dalton was trying to think about what kids talk about. "You got a bike?" he asked.

"Yeah. It has a flat tire though," Billy said.

"Oh. You know how to fix it?" Dalton asked.

"No. My Mom does though. She said when it gets warm we'll

fix it together," Billy said.

Dalton nodded.

"You like the snow?" Dalton asked.

"Yeah," Billy said. Again silence. Billy looked around the room.

"You have a nice home Mr. Jones."

Dalton smiled, and realized how mature Billy was trying to be—then again, maybe he was like this all the time. Dalton had never seen him act up like some kids. Dalton also noticed for the first time how much Billy looked like Angie.

"Did you build this house?" Billy asked.

"No," said Dalton, "My Dad built this place a long time ago."

"Where is he now?" Billy asked.

"Dead," Dalton said.

"I don't know my dad," Billy said.

Dalton felt a little uncomfortable, like they were starting to talk about a forbidden subject, and wasn't sure how to respond. "My mom doesn't ever talk about him, but I know I have one because it takes two people to make a baby." Dalton was squirming in his seat now—he looked around the room for a distraction.

"Want to help me feed the cat?" Dalton asked.

"Sure," Billy said, and followed Dalton back into the kitchen. He watched as Dalton put some dry food into a dish on the table. "How old are you, Mr. Jones?"

"Old."

"You got kids?"

"One."

"Boy or a girl?"

"Boy."

"Where is he?"

"New York."

"Does he ever come home?"

"Not very often."

"You have any friends?"

"A few," said Dalton.

"Are they old too?"

"Pretty old," said Dalton.

Billy stood there by the table watching Sam eat—trying to think of more questions when Meg came through the back door with a shopping bag in her arms.

"Hello William!" she said to Billy. Meg set the bag on the counter and shook Billy's hand. "I'm Dalton's big sister, Margaret, call me Meg."

"Nice to meet you ma'am," Billy said.

"Such a little gentleman," She said, and then began to unload the paper shopping bag full of food she'd prepared. Dalton and Billy sat down on both sides of the table and Meg moved Sam's food dish to the floor. The three of them sat and talked and ate lunch. Conversation was much easier with Meg there—she and Billy talked about school and his teachers. She asked how his grandmother was. They talked about summer, dogs, and for the most part Dalton just sat there, listening, and thinking what a good kid Billy was.

When they finished lunch, Meg gave Billy some cookies and milk, and he asked if he could watch TV. Dalton didn't care and showed him how to turn it on, and how to straighten the rabbit ear antenna's for better reception. "I only get a few channels," Dalton said.

"That's okay," Billy said as he climbed up onto the couch. Dalton went back into the kitchen where Meg was now wiping down the counters and table top with a wet dishrag. Dalton watched Sam saunter into the living room and jump up on the couch next to Billy. Dalton raised an eyebrow, Sam didn't usually warm up to people very quickly.

"Want some coffee?" Meg asked as Dalton sat down at the table.

"No," he said. Meg started sweeping the floor.

"You sure you don't want some coffee?"

"No, I'm fine," Dalton said. He sat there at the table wringing his hands—thinking he needed to tell Meg about the cancer. He didn't want to, but if anyone should know, Meg should. He'd always protected her by trying to keep the painful things from her. She seemed so fragile at times. He never wanted to hurt her—but he knew he had to tell her. He watched her empty the dustpan into the garbage and go back to sweeping the hard wood floor.

"Meg, there's something I need to talk to you about," Dalton said.

"What is it?" Meg said still sweeping the floor. "If this is about Sam, you know I'll watch him while your in New York. I always do. Are you getting excited about your trip?"

"It will be good to see Dan," Dalton said.

"You've decided to go to the lecture haven't you?" She stopped sweeping and smiled at Dalton. "We'll all have to ride together—gas is so expensive. It'll be so good to see Elizabeth again."

"I don't think I'll be going to the lecture Meg, I've been kind of tired."

"Your not coming down with something are ya? It's flu season, you know, and you didn't get a flu shot like I told you too."

"Meg, I'm sick," Dalton said. She stopped sweeping and looked up at her little brother.

"Coming down with a cold?" Meg asked.

"Meg," Dalton said gently, "I have cancer." Meg stood there clutching the broom. Her wide eyes filled with tears and her bottom lip began to quiver. She leaned the broom against the counter top, wiped her hands on the dish towel, and then sat down at the table across from Dalton. She sat there in silence as big tears began to stream down her cheeks.

"Cancer?" she said.

"I just found out. It started in the prostate, and has spread. I went and saw Aaron Mackenzie a few weeks ago because I was having back pain—I thought I pulled a muscle or some damn thing. He gave me a physical and did some blood work, and that led to more tests."

"Will you get a second opinion?" Meg whispered, wiping away tears.

"Aaron sent all the blood work and tests to the big hospital in Traverse City—so in a way I already have several opinions, all agreeing—I don't need another one." Dalton said, and reached across the table to take Meg's hand. She was trying to remain calm, to be supportive, but all she could do was cry.

"What will they do?" she asked.

Dalton hesitated, "Aaron said months ago they may have been able to operate, but the cancer has metastasized. He said if I do chemo and radiation it may prolong it."

"Prolong it—the cancer?" Meg asked.

"My life," Dalton said. "The cancer is real bad Meg—I don't have a long time."

"Oh Dalton," she said and covered her mouth with one hand, and with the other squeezed Dalton's hand so hard her knuckles turned white. "You'll do the chemo?"

"I don't know. I don't know if I want to go through all that if the end result is going to be the same."

"Oh Dalton, you have to—you just have to," she cried.

Dalton looked down at the table.

"Do it for me—please Dalton," Meg pleaded.

"Meg... I really don't know what I want to do. I need to think about all of this for a few days," he said. They sat there for a long time and he continued to hold her hand—he couldn't stand to see her cry. It reminded Dalton of when his cousin Edward died and he sat the same way talking to his mother, in the same kitchen, at the same table. "I love you Meg," Dalton said.

"I love you too," Meg replied.

Later, Billy fell asleep while watching television, and Meg sat in Dalton's chair and worked on crocheting a new afghan. Dalton covered Billy up with an old afghan Meg had made him several years before. He stood there looking at Billy and tried to remember when Dan was that age—but all the memories seemed so distant and vague. He turned off the television and went back into the kitchen, prepared himself a drink, and sat down at the kitchen table to write in his journal. He wrote about his parents, Meg, his cousin Edward, and of the fond memories he had of childhood. He wrote about this old house on Cathead Bay, and how he hoped it would stay in the family after he was gone. He wondered if he had—or ever would have grandchildren, and if they would know anything about him. Dalton stopped writing for a moment, leaned back in his chair, and sipped warm whiskey while pondering the thought of being a grandfather.

Angie was to get out of work at 4:00 P.M., so around 3:15 Dalton went out and cleared the snow off Meg's car, and the old truck. He started both vehicles and let them warm up for a little bit—blasting the defrosters. Inside Meg gathered her dishes, and Billy's coat, gloves, and bookbag. She helped him on with his coat, and they both met Dalton out in the driveway. Dalton hugged Meg goodbye, and thanked her for coming out. She said goodbye to Billy, and that she hoped to see him again real soon. Dalton helped Meg into her car, then Billy into the Truck. With the truck's headlights reflecting in Meg's rearview mirror—Dalton followed her down the long driveway, and into town.

As Meg drove home she cried, not only for Dalton or herself, but for the overall tragedy of this life. She cried for all the years of struggle, pain, and illness, for all the yearning and death, the lack of answers—and now this. How could she go on without Dalton? What would become of her life? She never dreamed that she'd be the last of her family. She had Charlie, and she knew he loved her—and she loved him—but often, even when he was near she felt so alone. Since she and Charlie never had children, Dalton had been the focus of her attention for many years, her baby brother had been the only constant in her life. Meg wasn't much for change, and didn't know if she could bare this loss.

Eleven

The next morning, back at the house on Cathead Bay, Dalton packed for his trip to New York. Sam watched from the corner of the room. He knew what the black bag meant and said nothing in protest. Dalton fumbled around the house for a while, avoiding the folded newspaper with Elizabeth's photo. He opened another bottle of whiskey and had a drink. He was feeling pretty good and decided to go for a walk along the lake shore. He dressed warm and went out the back door, stepping through the deep snow towards Cathead Bay. It was cold this morning and the sky was a crisp blue. Dalton's eyes watered as the cold wind blew. The low waves formed foaming white caps, and the tall beach grass waved back and forth. Dalton took a deep breath and walked the beach leaving behind a lone set of footprints as he wandered across the winter sand, north towards the Grand Traverse lighthouse along the lonesome wooded path. He listened to the sound of the waves and the breeze through the rustling pines. His eyes continued to water and his cheeks were cold and red. The further he walked, the more he hurt deep down in his back and groin. It took him almost a half an hour to get out by the lighthouse on the most northern point of the Leelanau Peninsula.

When he arrived he stood there on the beach looking as far off in the distance as he could see. It was a beautiful day. The sky and the water was so blue. Off in the distance a freighter passed, it moved slowly across the horizon, and then it was gone. Dalton stood there taking in deep breaths of cold air. He'd been thinking about Elizabeth Wharton all morning, trying to ignore the fact that she was giving her lecture this evening, but it was all he could think about.

Walking the shore back to the house, he recalled another time so long ago when he walked here with her. He took another breath of the cold air and pushed his hands deep into his pockets. Before he got back to the house, he knew he'd go to the lecture.

Later that day after a long nap and a little whiskey, Dalton put on a clean shirt and jeans, and combed his hair. He picked up the folded newspaper on his way out the door. He drove slowly through Northport and then on to Traverse City. He was two hours early, so he found a little tavern and had a drink. He sat at a table in the back to write in his journal, and thought about how he knew he deserved everything he'd got out of life—the loneliness, the empty home. He probably even deserved this damn cancer.

The first words he wrote in the journal were, *"Marriage was difficult for me…"* then he took a long drink of cold beer. He used to pray a lot, no one knew that—or could have guessed, but he prayed for hope, for purpose, and for a reason to carry his body through life. He took another drink of beer, and waved to the waitress for another. He felt a little out of place in this tavern, away from the Grandview and Northport—but the beer was cold and steady, and it was a comfortable place to write. Dalton thought if he were a character, and this were his story—what a somber sad story it would be up to this point. He thought about the early years when his son was born, and he'd already written the best-selling novel and was trying to recreate the magic. His second novel got bad reviews, leaving Dalton feeling that he wasn't very good at anything and the world was this big miserable place. He felt like everyone he encountered was unhappy, cynical and angry. But, in hindsight it was all inside himself. As for the second novel, it wasn't that the book wasn't any good, it was just that all the critics had loved the first novel so much, they were looking for a sequel, and that wasn't what Dalton had given them.

His third novel bombed as well, leaving him feeling that he couldn't write anymore, and the resurrection of old insecurities—that he wasn't that intelligent or intellectual. He'd always been a slow learner. He also wished he wasn't so damn empathetic and compulsive—life's not fair, and it is not easy. It's not all fun and games. There were no answers, only questions, fear, and a very faint sense of hope.

After Dalton and Lilly had been married for a few years, he published several short stories, then went to work on the fourth novel—working night and day, and he was happy and laughing all the time. For a short time he and Lilly were very happy. The night he finished the novel, he went to Lilly and watched her sleep. He woke her and made love with her, and this seemed to be the new beginning they both longed for. Dalton's novel was published, and with it, the big check that brought a down payment on their first home, just north of Manhattan, in Yonkers, along the Hudson River. Two months after they moved in, their son Dan was born.

Once in the new home, Dalton continued to write—these were the good days. Later that year he finished another novel, but the publisher rejected it. They said the only way they could accept it was if he rewrote entire chapters, and that there was major editing to be done. He took the criticism hard, and tried to rewrite what they asked for, but was stressed and felt like hell. He was overwhelmed with the publisher's request, and even though he attempted the rewrite, he'd secretly given up.

When Lilly asked how it was coming along he'd snap at her. Everything had been going so well, but Dalton was falling into that dark place. Lilly held her breath waiting for the other shoe to drop—it always did with Dalton.

One afternoon Lilly took Dan into New York City, and Dalton stayed home and got drunk. He starred out his window overlooking the Hudson River and the Palisades—watching the ships go by reminded him of Northport. His mind wandered, eventually taking him back to Elizabeth. He felt it was time to write her, to tell her he still thought about her.

He started the letter, but was too drunk to finish it, and decided to go for a walk along the river. When he arrived back home he found Lilly sitting on their bedroom floor crying. She told Dalton she read the letter. Dalton said nothing, turned, and walked away. He locked himself in his den and continued to drink.

Ironically, a few days later he received a letter from Elizabeth, and it said many of the same things he'd tried to say in his unfinished letter. After he read her letter, he sat alone in the dark den, wishing there was another way. He wanted to live this life so fully, to be productive and creative. He felt like he was drifting through life, and was filled with these overwhelming sensations of fear. He reread the letter from Elizabeth again, and imagined her there with him, and cried.

Dalton reread the line he'd wrote, *"Marriage was difficult for me..."* and looked up at the clock above the bar—he still had forty-five minutes until the lecture started. He ordered another beer and a double shot of whiskey.

He arrived at the university a little drunk but nobody would ever know it. People were beginning to move into the auditorium. He lingered in the hallway for a while looking for Charlie and Meg, then decided he really didn't want to see them if they were there. He walked down a dark hall, and passed the student bookstore where there were signs posted everywhere for a used book sale. He didn't see any of his books, only some classics like *Candide, The Sun Also Rises, The Grapes of Wrath*, and there was Kerouac's *On the Road*—how the college curriculum had changed, Dalton thought. He picked up an old dog-eared paperback of *Dear Theo* by Vincent Van Gogh. It had been years since Dalton had read it. He flipped it open to a page folded almost in half, there was an entire paragraph highlighted, it read, *"One must especially have the end in mind, and the victory one would gain after a whole life of work and effort, is better than one that is gained earlier."* Towards the bottom of the page another highlighted paragraph, *"Whoever lives sincerely and encounters much trouble and disappointment, but is not bowed down by them, is worth more than the one who has always sailed before the wind and has always known relative prosperity. One must never trust the occasion when one is without difficulties."* Dalton reread that last line a couple more times and tossed the book back into the bin of used books.

He walked back to the auditorium. Everyone was seated. When he heard the voice of Elizabeth Wharton, his heart started pounding. He thought about turning around, but he found a seat in the back row where he could go unseen. By chance he noticed Charlie and Meg about seven or eight rows in front of him. Elizabeth spoke for an hour about creative energy, about the left and right hemispheres of the brain, and the need for balance, a blending of the two hemispheres. She walked back and forth across the stage and was very engaging and animated. She was heavier, older, and wore her silver hair up, and her glasses rested on the end of her nose. She made her way back towards the middle of the stage and ended the lecture with, "Creative people think they are creative, and imagine success. Many of us give ourselves a reason, or an excuse to fail, but if we think we are creative we will be—it's habit! Listen to your inner voice! Thank you ladies and gentleman."

The light started to come on, and the crowd began to applaud and to stand up. Elizabeth said, "I'll be around for a few minutes if anyone has any more questions or comments—or just want to say hello."

Dalton was the first to leave the auditorium, pushing through the crowd towards the door. He wanted to avoid Charlie and Meg, and didn't want Elizabeth to see him. He was close to the door when a woman in a grey suit stepped in front of him.

"Mr. Jones?" She said. Dalton froze.

"Yes?" he said. She stuck out her hand.

"I'm the chairman of the art department here at the University— I just had to say hello—I'm such a fan of your work," She said while still pumping his hand. Dalton was distracted, glancing to his left and right. He thanked her, smiled, excused himself, and then quickly left the building.

He sat in the cab of his truck for about ten minutes contemplating going back inside, but when it came right down to it—it had been so long, and he didn't want to see Elizabeth just to tell her he was dying. Perhaps this was an old story best left unresolved.

Back inside Meg and Charlie made their way down to the

stage and waited for Elizabeth to finish a conversation with a young woman. When through, she turned and saw Meg and Charlie standing there. Meg was beaming.

"Margaret!" Elizabeth said, surprised. They embraced for a long time, and Meg cried. Elizabeth embraced Charlie, then turned back to Meg and took her hands. "How are you?"

"Oh, fine," Meg said, wiping tears. "Older, fatter."

"Aren't we all," Elizabeth said and they both laughed.

"Where have the years gone?" Meg said in a long sigh.

"Time has gone by so quickly," Elizabeth said.

"You're teaching at the university now?" Meg asked.

"Yes," said Elizabeth. "I have been for some time."

"So you live in Mt. Pleasant?" Meg asked.

"No," and there was a brief uncomfortable pause, "I live in Midland, with my husband."

"Oh," Meg said. "I didn't know you married again."

"It's been a long time Meg," Elizabeth said, and squeezed Meg's hand. A tear rolled down Meg's cheek.

"We tried to get Dalton to come this evening, but he wasn't feeling up to it," Meg said.

Elizabeth smiled politely.

"We had some bad news this week Elizabeth. Dalton has cancer."

Elizabeth didn't know what to say. She felt indifferent with the news. It had been so many years, so much time at a distance—separating her life from their's. It had taken her years to build these walls protecting herself from painful memories of the past. She wanted to feel something more—anything—but there was nothing, only an emptiness where there should have been emotion. She felt cold, and sorry for Meg, but that was all.

Charlie felt uncomfortable with Meg talking about Dalton's cancer so soon, but there was nothing he could do.

"It's prostate cancer," Meg cried. "It's real bad, I guess."

"Is his family with him?" Elizabeth asked. Meg glanced to Charlie, then back to Elizabeth.

"No. He and Lilly were divorced some time ago, she and Dan are both back in New York."

"Oh, I didn't know," Elizabeth said. As much as she felt for Meg, she was beginning to feel uncomfortable and anxious talking about Dalton. "Are you still in Northport?"

"Same old house," Meg said. "Were not far from Dalton, so we are there for him."

"Thank God he has you both," Elizabeth said.

Meg noticed several other people who stepped up to the side of Elizabeth, hoping to talk to her.

"Oh, we better not take up all of your time," Meg said. "I'd really love to get together for coffee or tea one of these days."

"I would like that too, Meg," Elizabeth sincerely smiled. "We need to do that." The two women hugged and Meg cried a little more. They promised they would get together soon, and Meg and Charlie left the auditorium.

Once Elizabeth had spoken with everyone who had waited around to see her, she picked up her coat and purse and started up the steps of the auditorium. When she reached the top of the stairs the chairman of the art department came rushing up to her.

"You were just wonderful tonight Ms. Wharton," she beamed.

"Thank you," Elizabeth said while buttoning up her coat.

"You will never guess who was here tonight?"

"Whose that? Elizabeth asked, wrapping her scarf around her neck.

"Dalton Jones. The author."

Elizabeth must have looked like she saw a ghost.

"Are you all right Ms. Wharton?" the chairman asked.

"Oh, yes, I'm sorry—just a little tired," Elizabeth smiled, but the wall of indifference she felt when talking to Meg had cracked.

"Well, isn't it exciting that he would come to the University for our event—I'm such a huge fan of his." The Chairman smiled, and Elizabeth smiled back, while glancing around to see if Dalton was still here. "He left in such a hurry, probably afraid of being noticed," The chairman said, still grinning.

"I'm sure," Elizabeth said, relieved Dalton was gone. She thanked the chairman again, and said goodbye. Out in the parking lot she glanced around nervously for Dalton as her husband, Roger, pulled up in their car to meet her. As she climbed in and put on her seat belt, she let out a deep sigh.

"You did a great job tonight honey," Roger said. She smiled and looked a little pale. "You okay?" he asked.

"Yes," she said. "Just tired." She needed to get away, someplace safe and far away from the resurfacing past—back to her calm, happy life. She closed her eyes, and Roger adjusted the heater and drove her home to Midland.

Twelve

It was 11:46 P.M. Dalton sat down at the kitchen table with a glass of ice and poured warm whiskey over it. He'd turned on one light there in the kitchen. It was quiet. Sam was already asleep upstairs. Dalton was packed and ready to leave the following morning for New York. When he got home he went upstairs and pulled out a box of old journals he kept in his closet, so many details from the past were vague, faded memories. He wanted more clarity before he saw Lilly. This very well may be the last time he'd ever see her, and he wanted to say something meaningful.

He took the journals back downstairs and at the kitchen table. He turned their pages remembering their home in Yonkers overlooking the Hudson River, and their son growing up, and thought about how much he missed out on. Dalton was there the entire time, but missed so much during those years by being consumed with himself. What should have been the best time of his life had escaped him. Back then he held Lilly accountable for a good portion of his misery, but looking back, he knew it was his fault. All she ever did was try. He couldn't see that then. He took a drink. The ice was melting. There was condensation on the glass and his fingers were wet as he opened another old journal…

June 17, Yonkers New York

Been a few weeks since I put my thoughts down in a clear voice. I suppose a clear voice needs a clear mind. A few nights ago I lay in the tub drinking whiskey. I've been taking prescribed pills—and I know I shouldn't be while drinking—but I did. Later emerging from the tub—only to wake up in bed in a pool of my own vomit. Lilly removed the sheets, and I was back in the shower, then slept on the bathroom floor wrapped in a towel. I woke in the morning and fought my way through the day. My writing stops completely when I go through this—I see how counter productive it is. It stagnates me, slows me down and feeds the depression. I never thought of myself as the type who couldn't handle it—I realize I may have a bit of an addictive personality.

Dalton took another drink and turned the page.

July 1, Yonkers New York
I've been getting good feedback from the last novel. It's brought many tears, laughter, envy, and so on—feels good to be finished with it and to have it spread around. Every one's happy for me, but Lilly. She smiles, while coveting me for her own cruel intentions. I remain silent here in the dark, with pen in hand. These words are all I truly have left to express the light that burns from within.

Dalton turned a few pages…

October 14
I haven't spoke to Elizabeth in over a year. After so much talk, and letters, I have no idea where she is, what she's doing. There was a moment in time I thought we would be perfect for one another, but then there was a great hesitation, and that fog never cleared—and she faded away. I never wrote her back after the last letter. I couldn't. I had to stop talking to her. The last few times we corresponded I could tell she was angry and confused. She was trying to get on with her life, while I was still hanging on.

Dalton closed the journal and finished his drink.

Different days—but it all sounded the same. So much time had passed, it was all blurred together, and he had forgotten the day-to-day struggles. If he were a younger man, he'd be sad, distraught even—but Dalton didn't have time for that now. He didn't really understand everything that was happening concerning the cancer, or how much time he actually had left. He was uncomfortable, but the pain was bearable—in an unbearable sort of way.

He shut off the kitchen light and went up to his bedroom. As he passed he and Lilly's wedding portrait that still was hanging in his room, he paused and straightened the frame on the wall. Sam was asleep on the bed as Dalton undressed and crawled between the cold sheets. He wasn't quite ready for sleep as he lay there listening to the wind rattle his bedroom windows, so he decided to read. He had a stack of books next to the bed, reached down, and accidently knocked them over. He fumbled for whatever he could reach without getting out of bed, and picked up an old paperback version of *Town and the City* by Jack Kerouac. He looked at the cover for a moment and thought about the one and only time he met Kerouac. It was sixty-something, and they were all drinking in a little bar in Greenwich Village. Dalton knew who Kerouac was, but Jack had no idea who Dalton was. Dalton recalled how envious, and in awe he was of Kerouac at the time. Dalton had read *Town and the City* several times, and this copy was written in, underlined, and pages dog-eared. Dalton thought this was one of Kerouac's great books, and so often overlooked, overshadowed by some of his later work. Dalton flipped through the pages, and started to read passages he'd underlined a long time ago.

The last one he read before closing his eyes was on page 234; it said, *"And he was sick now with crying lonesomeness, he somehow knew that all moments were farewell, all life was goodbye."*

Thirteen

Dalton woke up early. He took a hot bath and drank a little whiskey. When he got out of the tub he dressed, gathered his bags, and a couple more old journals to read while on the plane. He called Meg to say he was off, and said goodbye to Sam. In the old truck he drove to Traverse city, the roads were dry and clear.

He left his truck in the airport parking lot and caught his flight to Detroit. He had a two-hour layover, and then caught the connecting flight to LaGuardia. By the time he got off the plane and collected his bags it was about 3:45 P.M. He went outside and stood in line for a cab. It was cold, but not as cold as Northport. When it was his turn he climbed in the back of a yellow cab.

"Where to?" the cab driver asked with a thick accent Dalton didn't recognize.

"East Village, 4th Street, between First and Second," Dalton said.

The cabby hit the gas and pulled out away from the airport. In a moment they were on the Grand Central Parkway—it was stop and go, changing lanes.

"Visiting?" the cabby said.

"My son," said Dalton.

"First time to New York?"

"No," Dalton said. "I lived here a long time ago."

"Where you from?" The cabby asked, speeding up, slowing down, and occasionally glancing in the rearview mirror.

"Michigan," Dalton said.

"How far?"

"Driving—about twelve hours, by plane—two or three." The cabby nodded. They drove along in silence for a few moments, merged onto the Brooklyn Queens expressway. Traffic lightened up a little until they got on the LIE—then it was slow until they got through the tunnel and emerged in Mid-town. They flew down 2nd Avenue, through a couple of red lights, and around some pedestrians. In just a few more minutes they were in the East Village, and a quick left on 4th Street.

"Anywhere along here is fine," Dalton said, and the driver pulled over to the right and stopped the meter. Dalton paid, gave him a good tip, and stepped out of the cab onto 4th Street. The cab driver jumped out and got Dalton's bag from the trunk. Dalton thanked him, then the cab disappeared into a sea of yellow cabs heading East down the one-way street.

Dalton put his bag strap over his shoulder and started walking down the block to Dan's apartment. It was about 4:30 now; he was a little early, but that was all right. He walked the tree-lined street, and thought about how the East Village had changed over the past twenty years. Dalton had heard a lot of the old-timers complain about the changes... the *gentrification*—but the place was cleaned up. The drugs and homelessness was less apparent, and people felt safe walking around after dark again. The people who have always flocked to the East Village seemed the same, that bohemian element, creative— desperate to live their lives—young people.

The East Village wasn't a place for Dalton anymore—he'd lost that sense of urgency that once filled him. He'd lived too long, lost too much, been beaten too far down. Today he was just happy to exist, and now even that was in jeopardy.

He walked up to Dan's building, no steps, just a black iron security door with scratched Plexiglas where the glass use to be. He rang the buzzer for apartment 7—which was on the top floor of this 100-year-old 4th floor walk up. The ground level was an Indian restaurant, and due to poor ventilation, the entire building smelled like curry. Dalton rang the buzzer again, but there was still no answer. He looked at his watch, 4:45—still forty-five minutes early. Dan had told him they could all meet at his apartment at 5:30. Dalton stepped away from the building and looked down the street for a bar. He didn't see anything, so he walked down 4th Street to Avenue A, took a left towards Tompkins Square Park—he was sure there were still a few places to get a drink over there. He walked past a couple bars, waiting for one to jump out at him. He went a few blocks, and there was this one on the corner that had a chalk portrait of Johnny Cash on the exterior wall. "There it is," Dalton said out loud to himself and went inside. He bellied up to the bar where there was a handsome young woman pouring beers. She made eye contact with Dalton—that was as good as a hello in New York.

"Double shot of whiskey—no ice," Dalton said. She nodded, and put the glass in front of him. He was hurting, and wondered how long would he be able to bear the pain.

He checked his watch, still time.

He kept looking out the window—watching the traffic and the people passing by. He understood the draw the East Village had on Dan, and if he were a younger man, he'd probably come back here himself.

He finished his drink and ordered another—finished that one and it was about time. He left a big bill on the counter and nodded to the bartender as he stepped away. It took him about ten minutes to get back to Dan's apartment, and this time when he rang the buzzer, Dan's voice came over the intercom.

"Yes?" Dan said.

"It's Dad," he said. Dan buzzed open the door, Dalton swung the heavy security door open and started up the stairs of the old narrow hallway, dirty and dim light—smelled like curry from the Indian restaurant on the first floor. He took it one step at a time, head down, breathing. It seemed like a long way to the top. When he got to the top floor the door to apartment 7 was open a crack. Dalton could hear the voice of Walter Covington, Lilly's new husband—he was a loud guy, always talking, never had anything to say.

Dalton knocked on the door and Dan swung it open.

"Hi dad!" he said, and they shook hands. "Come on in." Dan took Dalton's bag and motioned for him to step in further. Lilly and Walter were both there, both silent, expressionless for a brief moment, and then Walter stepped forward.

"Hello Dalton, good to see you!" They shook hands and Dalton nodded, forced a smile.

"Hello Dalton," Lilly said, standing back. The wine in her glass was motionless. She looked beautiful—she always did.

"You keep getting younger, Lilly—and I keep getting older," Dalton said. She smiled, and said nothing.

"Can I get you something to drink Dad?"

"Sure."

Dan disappeared into a small closet of a kitchen. There was another awkward silence between Dalton, Lilly and Walter. From the back room Dan's girlfriend emerged—flipping her hair back. She had a drink in one hand. When she saw Dalton, she got all excited, ran up and shook his hand.

"I'm Julie—I've been so anxious to meet you—I'm such a huge fan. I can't believe you came all this way for my opening!" Dan came from the kitchen and handed Dalton a drink.

"Don't scare him off Julie," Dan said.

"Nice to meet you Julie," Dalton said. "Congratulations on the big art show."

"I just finished your last book," she said standing way too close to Dalton. He didn't take it personally; she was from New York and didn't know any better. People from the mid-west need more space, and Dalton took a casual step back, and a sip of his drink.

"I've got so many questions for you about the ending," Julie said. Dalton thought she was relentless, and was feeling trapped when Dan finally interrupted.

"Well, is everyone about ready for dinner?" he said. "I thought we could walk down the street to the *B Bar and Grill*, a little place we like, then just catch a cab over to the gallery after." Julie was a little drunk already, and this remark easily distracted her. When she turned towards Dan, she spilled her drink on her blouse.

"Mother fucker!" she said. Everyone was startled. "I have to change," and she went back to the bedroom. Lilly and Walter exchanged judgemental glances. Dan excused himself as well and followed her back to the bedroom and shut the door behind him.

"Can you please not bother my Dad about his book," Dan said. "I told you he's a little stand-offish. She gave Dan a dirty look as she took off her blouse.

"Fuck off, I wasn't bothering him—you need to calm down, you've been freaking out all day."

"Can you just slow down a little bit—you're already drunk, and you have a long night ahead of you."

"I don't need a god damn baby sitter Dan. Are you embarrassed of me?"

"Tonight is a big night for you—for us. I don't want you to make an ass out of yourself and regret it in the morning. Besides the show, I want my parents to walk away feeling good about us," Dan said.

After Dan and Julie stepped into the bedroom, there was silence again between Dalton, Lilly and Walter. Dalton sipped his drink and Walter's cell phone rang. He took it out of his pocket, "It's Steven," he said to Lilly. "My son," he said to Dalton. "I'm going to step outside and take this." Lilly nodded and Walter left the apartment and went downstairs to the small courtyard behind the building.

Dalton and Lilly stood there for a moment still silent.

"How have you been?" Lilly asked.

"Fine," Dalton said.

"You look like hell," Lilly said. Dalton smiled and lifted his glass to her. "Looks like you have quite the fan in Julie."

"Seems that way," Dalton said, glancing around the apartment.

"It's not serious," Lilly said.

"What's that?"

"Dan and Julie—it won't last."

"Oh?" Dalton said with raised eyebrows, and then took another drink. "I was under the impression they were pretty serious."

"I read the book too," Lilly said. "It was good. I didn't see why you had to kill the main character—a meaningless ending."

"Life's that way sometimes," Dalton said.

"Well, it was good—I didn't think you still had it in you," Lilly said, then sipped her wine, leaving lipstick on the rim of the glass. Dalton noticed the diamond on her finger.

"Good god, that's a hell of a rock—I thought you didn't like jewelry?"

"It was a gift from Walter for our tenth anniversary," Lilly said, looking at the ring indifferently.

"Has it been that long?" Dalton said.

"Times goes fast," Lilly said, then silence. "How are Meg and Charlie?"

"Fine, nothing new."

"How about you—seeing anyone?" Lilly asked. Dalton smiled.

"No. Just me and old Sam in that big house."

"I can't believe you still have that cat—you always acted like you hated it."

"Well," Dalton said, "we sort of grew on one another." He imagined what Sam could be doing at this very moment—probably sprawled out across the kitchen table waiting for Meg to bring him dinner. Lilly walked over to the kitchen counter and poured herself a little more wine. Dalton watched her move across the room.

Walter came back into the apartment.

"Well, Steven sends his love and said he wished he could have been here," Walter said to Lilly. Dalton often forgot that his kid has had step siblings for the last ten years. Dan never mentioned them to Dalton, but Dalton knew they saw one another quite often. "So Dalton," Walter said, picking up his drink, "between you and me, how much did you pull in on this last book? I saw it was on the *New York Times* best seller list—I bet your making a pretty penny—gimme a number?"

"Oh Walt," Dalton said. He called him Walt because he knew he preferred to be called Walter, "you know I don't handle all that."

But Dalton did know—he knew exactly.

"Well, I bet it's a lot," Walter said. "You really should have a better handle on all that stuff—there are people out there who prey on folks like you—the trusting type."

"That so," Dalton said, insulted and amused at the same time.

"All right boys," Lilly said—interrupting, knowing full well that Dalton was baiting Walter. Dan and Julie came back out of the bedroom. She seemed to have calmed down, and changed into a new blouse. Dan now had on a tie and jacket. Dalton thought for a moment that he might be a little under dressed—but then, he didn't really care.

"Well—is everyone hungry?" Dan asked. They were, and they all started to file down the stairs to the street. Before Dan locked the apartment, Dalton pulled one of the smaller old journals he'd brought with him out of his bag and stuck it in his back pocket. They all made it down to the street, and started toward the Bowery, to the *B Bar and Grill* on 4th Street—between Lafayette and Broadway.

It wasn't too cold tonight—just comfortable to walk a few blocks. They all made small talk along the way, and Dan was trying hard to keep both his parents engaged in conversation. They made it to the restaurant, got drinks at the bar, and were seated. Dalton made sure to sit at the end, next to Dan, and not Julie. Walter sat across from Dalton in the booth, and for Dan's sake alone Dalton pretended to be interested in what Walt had to say throughout dinner.

Dalton had a big steak—medium-rare, a baked potato smothered in butter and sour cream, fresh asparagus. They all had a few more drinks. Watching Julie, Dalton thought that for a little thing she could really pack away the booze, but she was becoming noticeably more drunk and loud. Walt insisted on picking up the tab—Dalton graciously accepted. Besides, he figured Walt was sleeping with his wife; the least he could do was buy Dalton dinner every once in a while.

Julie whispered something to Dan, and he shook his head—then she spoke up, "Dan has something to tell everyone!"

"No," he said—not tonight," Dan said.

"What's the news Dan? Walter said.

"Tell them!" Julie squealed. Dan looked down, then to his mother.

"Well, Julie and I have been talking about getting married."

Lilly almost choked on her drink, "Married?" she said.

Dalton said nothing.

"Isn't that wonderful!" Julie said. "My mother and I have already started planning the wedding—it's going to be wonderful—just wonderful." Dalton's gaze kept shifting from Lilly, to Dan—neither of them were saying anything, but their silence spoke volumes.

Walt finally crumbled, "Well that's wonderful—congratulations you two!" Lilly shot him a dirty look—then looked across the table at Dalton, who was grinning at her panicked expression—but she quickly pulled out of it, and turned back towards Julie and said, "Congratulations dear," then looked straight at Dan and said, "I had no idea."

"We haven't set a date or anything yet—we still have some time before…" Dan began,

"Yes, but we're engaged—we just have to pick out rings!" Julie interrupted.

The waitress brought back Walt's credit card and receipt. They all got up from the table—Walt helped the girls with their coats. Dan was looking a little anxious, Dalton patted him on the back, but didn't say a thing. They walked out front, to the corner of 4th Street and Bowery, and Walter hailed a cab. They all started to climb in, but Dan hesitated when he saw there wasn't enough room for everyone.

"Go ahead," Dalton said, "I'll catch the next one—you've got to get over there."

"You know where you're going?" Dan asked, and Dalton pulled the invitation to tonight's event out of his breast pocket and smiled. Dan hesitated, and then got in the cab. Dalton watched it pull away, and just stood there for a moment taking a couple deep breaths. Then he hailed another cab coming down Bowery—it pulled up, and he climbed in.

The cab driver was a young man; after Dalton closed the door they made eye contact through the rear-view mirror.

"Broadway and Spring Street," Dalton said, the driver hit the gas, and sped off down Bowery, then took a quick right onto Houston Street.

"Nice night," the driver said.

"Yeah," said Dalton, watching all the people out as they passed Elizabeth Street, Mott Street, and Mulberry. The driver confidently ran a red light on Lafayette, and then came to a stop at the intersection of Broadway.

"Going to a party?" the driver asked, his eyes were darting back and forth between the rear-view mirror and the traffic light.

"Of sorts, an art opening."

"You an artist?"

"Well, no," Dalton said. "It's for my son's girlfriend."

"Ah, you're being a good father! That's good, that's good!" The light turned green, he quickly changed lanes, and made a left onto Broadway. As soon as it was clear he hit the gas. They flew past a crowd of people eager to cross Prince Street, and in seconds they were at Spring Street and Broadway. The cabby, hit his brakes, threw on his blinker, and pulled up next to some parked cars. Dalton read the meter, handed the guy some cash, with a healthy tip.

"Thanks," Dalton said.

"Thank you, enjoy the show," the driver said. Dalton climbed out and shut the door. He stepped between the parked cars up to the sidewalk on Broadway. He pulled the invitation out of his pocket again to remind him what the address was, walked a few steps, turned the corner onto Spring Street, and then started towards the gallery.

The gallery was crowded; there was a huge turn out for the show. When Dan and Julie walked in, they scanned the crowd for people they knew. Lilly and Walter came in behind them. Julie's art dealer, Tabitha Washington, waved at her from across the room, and they started making their way towards one another.

"Hello Darling," Julie said to Tabitha. "This is my fiancé, Dan Jones." Dan shook her hand, and Julie watched Dan's eyes to see how he looked at Tabitha. Julie was extremely jealous.

Dan introduced Lilly and Walter to Tabitha—they all smiled and made brief conversation. Tabitha leaned towards Julie; "The press is here—someone from the *Village Voice*, there are a couple more, I'm not sure where they are from—be sure to introduce yourself and talk to them all."

Julie nodded, and moved off into the crowd, leaving Dan, Lilly and Walter standing there in a sea of people. Lilly looked around the room at Julie's work and thought it was interesting. Had it not been Julie's art Lilly would have like it even more. Walt had no opinion; he just stood there with his hands in his pockets, smiling—still thinking that he probably tipped the waitress too much at dinner. After a few minutes of standing there in the middle of the room, Dan led them all over to the bar for drinks. Walt was impressed that it was an open bar, and changed his order from a beer, to scotch and water.

Dalton came in through the front door and made his way through the crowd. He noticed that the majority of the crowd was young people. He looked around—a few sculptures, mostly oversized paintings. He saw Lilly standing by the bar, and he headed that way. Dan was there too, talking to Walter, pointing at one of the paintings. Dalton was almost over to Dan and Lilly when a young woman stepped in front of him and took his picture with a digital camera. The flash stopped Dalton—"Mr. Jones?" the young lady said, "Can I ask you a few questions?" Dan and Lilly were both watching this a few steps away.

"No—no, not tonight," Dalton said.

"Just a couple questions, sir—how do you feel about the attention your new book is getting?" She asked, and took another picture. This young reporter was starting to make a scene, and people were starting to notice—and whisper, *"Is that Dalton Jones?" "That's the author Dalton Jones,"* and Dalton was becoming uncomfortable.

Julie was across the room talking to the reporter from the *Village Voice* when the reporter noticed something was happening, and he excused himself while Julie was mid-sentence and headed over towards Dalton, who now had a small crowd gathering around him. Lilly was standing next to Dan watching all the commotion, then turned to Dan—she could see the envy and frustration in his eyes. She knew that it had been hard for Dan to try to make a name for himself being the son of a famous author. They were big shoes to fill, in some ways, Lilly thought. Lilly took Dan by the arm, "You okay?"

"Yeah," Dan said, watching his Dad—wanting to be his Dad, "I'm fine, but Julie is pissed." That didn't seem to matter as much to Lilly.

Dalton excused himself from the reporters, and headed towards the rest rooms in the back of the gallery. He had to walk past Lilly and Dan to get there, and grinned sheepishly as he went by. Lilly watched as Dalton zigzagged through the crowd, and slipped out the back door into the alley.

Fourteen

Dalton's breath was like fog around him in the dark alley. He pushed his hands into his jeans pockets—it was getting colder, or maybe he was just sobering up. He looked in both directions, chose one and disappeared into the shadows of Lower Manhattan.

He didn't have to go far to find a comfortable place to be—about a block to this little hole-in-the wall bar. It was full, but not crowded. Dalton went in, sat at an open spot at the end of the bar, and ordered a drink. He looked at his watch, maybe he would go back to the show—maybe he wouldn't. It was a tough call. He probably shouldn't have come at all, but he had too. He'd hoped to have a better opportunity to talk to Lilly. He couldn't say the things he needed to say to her in front of Walt. He was a good husband for her, but a dumb ass. Maybe the chance to talk to her would arise later tonight—maybe it wouldn't.

He thought about the night before—had he stuck around the University he would've had the chance to talk to Elizabeth—but trying to have that conversation with her with all those people around, would've been as uncomfortable as having a conversation with Walter. If he was going to talk to her, she needed fair warning, just showing up after all these years would be hard on them both. He wondered what her life ended up like, and if she was happy. He wondered what her reaction would've been had she seen him, and was there really anything left to say?

Besides all the correspondence through letters, Dalton and Elizabeth only saw each another a few times over the last fifteen or twenty years. One of those times was at the funeral of Dalton's father, Daniel Augustus Jones, everyone knew him as *Gus*. It was before the service when he saw Elizabeth. Prior to the funeral, the last time Dalton saw her she was falling asleep next to him in a cheap motel in Traverse City. And seeing her again at the funeral brought back so much unresolved emotion. Dalton made his way over to her, and tried to make small talk. He wondered if she could sense the heartache he was feeling—could she see the pain he was in, and the feelings he'd keep locked away. Unresolved emotion can destroy an individual, especially someone like Dalton who needed closure to everything— symbolic, ceremonial closure. Seeing Elizabeth at his father's funeral instantly took him back to that morning in the motel, to the moment he woke up and she was gone.

After the funeral, most everyone went to the Grandview for one last drink in honor of old Gus. Lilly had told Dalton she didn't think it was a good idea to take Dan to a bar, and took him home to Cathead Bay.

Dalton was one of the last to make it to the Grandview, and was standing at the bar when he noticed Elizabeth sitting alone at a table. He went to her and sat across from her, and that was the beginning of a conversation that lasted the rest of the evening. They talked of family, careers, creativity, and location. She asked about Lilly and Dan. Dalton was brief in his answers, glazing over the fact that he and Lilly were having problems, that Lilly was unhappy, that he was sad, and unful- filled with his life, career. He always felt like there should've been a little more laughter, passion, motivation, and love in life.

Dalton wanted to tell her he felt like he was just going through the motions, keeping himself anesthetized with alcohol. Lilly had all her organizations and clubs to fill her time, and she recently began talking about going back to work, which Dalton encouraged mostly to have the house to himself. Since his father's health began to worsen, they had spent more time in Northport, and he even suggested that he and Lilly sell the house in Yonkers and move back to Michigan full time. Lilly wasn't interested, but entertained the idea for Dalton's sake.

It was a bleak time in Dalton's life, but he didn't mention all that to Elizabeth. He didn't want to talk, he just wanted to listen to her, he always enjoyed listening to her. It was as if everyone else disappeared, and their conversation went on until late in the evening.

As the sun set, they stepped out of the Grandview, and walked together down to the marina. It was cool and he gave her his sport coat, placing it over her delicate shoulders. Dalton thought how she hadn't changed at all, still so sweet, kind, and beautiful. If she only knew how he was feeling. If he could only tell her. He wanted to hold her so badly, but didn't dare. They stood there on the docks of the marina, looking out over Grand Traverse Bay, watching the ducks move slowly through the water. She told Dalton that everything had its place and time, and that she felt like he was searching for something. He knew she was right, he thought it was her.

They walked back to the Grandview, where they said goodbye. Most of everyone else had left, and they stood there under the lights out front. Dalton desperately wanted to take her somewhere, to make love to her, to hold her, but knew it was too late, and that time had passed long ago. They said their awkward goodbye, embraced, and she turned and walked to her car. As she pulled away, she waved at Dalton, who was still standing there alone under the lights of the Grandview.

Dalton drove home and sat on the front porch until sunrise. He drank a few beers, smoked a few cigarettes, and waited for the sun to come up through the white pines. He finally went to bed that morning, and as he drifted off to sleep, he imagined a new life with Elizabeth, and all the things he would say to her, all the long conversations.

The next day Dalton locked up the house on Cathead Bay, drove Lilly and Dan to the airport in Traverse City, and they all flew back to New York. Dalton was silent all morning—during the drive, while making their way through the airport, and the flight home—he wanted to cry. He hurt so bad inside.

That was all a long time ago Dalton thought, sitting there at the end of that bar in lower Manhattan. He pulled his journal out of his pocket, with his sleeve he wiped the wet surface of the bar in front of him, then set the journal down. He opened it up and started turning the pages to where he'd left off reading earlier.

September 12, New York

"I know how much Lilly loves me, it would be hard to walk away from her. If I did it would alter our lives forever. I feel like the lousiest person there ever was."

Dalton sat there at the bar, turning the pages of the old journal. The people around him had left, he ordered another drink and continued reading.

September 14, New York, 12:45 A.M.

"I'm noticing patterns in my life—denial, reality, denial, reality—it's as simple as that. Lilly suggested I go see a shrink—but that's just another way to dilute the entire thing, like adding coke to whiskey—why bother. Lilly and I sat in a restaurant tonight, people all around, and I just felt so sad and alone. Friends and loved ones so far away.

I was at the Metropolitan Museum of Art the other day looking at the Van Gogh paintings, thinking about his life and death. He must have thought of his death as a transition, as if he'd gone as far as he could in this life. I'd probably do the same thing if I didn't feel like there was still something to live for—something I needed to do. Lilly keeps urging me to talk to the psychiatrist, its funny she doesn't like it when I'm drunk, but she's okay with me going and getting a prescription to some hard drugs that will alter my emotions and mind. I only see that road as yet another downward spiral. I've been drinking everyday because I don't have anything else. The older I get all I see around me is chaos and disorder running rampant—I see people dying, old people alone in the cold, homeless on the streets pissing themselves for a moment of warmth—dead birds on the sidewalks. I'm not as wistful as I once was, hell, even a few years ago, it's not all leading up to one big thing—well,

*death maybe—it's just going and going, and I get up every morning and
go, go, go, like a hamster on a wheel."*

Dalton ordered another drink and looked around the bar. He
thought going through these old journals was depressing as hell. He
turned the page and taped inside was a letter from Elizabeth—it was
a short letter that came as a response to a late night drunken poem
he'd sent her. When he sobered up he regretted sending it, but it
was the sad truth.

Her response read...

*"Dalton, I feel for you and the situation you find yourself in. I have
moved on in my life—I have met someone, and am happy. I see now that
he is a beautiful soul whom I love deeply. It seems that you are deeply unhappy and I wish for you the freedom that you need. The truth of how you
feel should be addressed so you can be at peace. Please do not contact me
again. I wish you the best as you make the choices that will set you free.
Sincerely, –Elizabeth."*

She also had sent back his poem, it was taped on the next page.
He opened it up, it was titled *Another Dream of You*. He read a little,
and then closed the journal. He'd read enough tonight to remember
some of the reasons why Lilly left him. His drunken depression had
gone on for a long time—usually in-between novels. Lilly lived with it
for a long time, and eventually had to leave.

After his father's death, Dalton convinced Lilly to spend half
the year in Northport and the other half in Yonkers. Initially she
agreed because Dalton said he'd be able to write better in Michigan,
and for several years they traveled back and forth. Lilly and Meg got
to be pretty good friends, but Lilly never really felt like she belonged
in Northport. She was a city girl and would go a little stir crazy
when she spent too much time in Northport. She usually ended up
spending a lot of time in Traverse City. She tried hard to make it all
work, but the more Dalton drank and carried on—the more alone

and miserable she was. She started spending less and less time in Michigan, and more time back in New York, leaving Dalton alone in Northport. Besides, it seemed like they got along better the less time they spent together. Even when she was with him, she felt like she was alone. He was always quiet and sad. Eventually she reached a point where she didn't know what to do—she loved Dalton, but wasn't *in love* with him anymore.

Dalton knew that while Lilly was in New York, she stayed very socially active, attended parties, went out with friends. She later confided in Dalton that one night while at a friend's birthday gathering was where she met Walter Covington for the first time. She said he was mature, well dressed, handsome—and single. A widower. He was very polite and interested in her. When he was talking to her, she said she kept twisting her wedding ring around her finger—hoping he wouldn't notice it. She was starved for attention. Walter asked if he could see her again and she said yes. That night she went home and called Dalton—but he didn't answer the phone, and she cried herself to sleep.

Dalton knew that after all the years she so desperately had tried to love him, she just couldn't do it anymore. Lilly was still young and attractive, and wanted to live her life. With Dalton she was sad and overlooked, their relationship had changed, and she knew in her heart that the marriage was over.

It was in the following weeks that she told Dan she was leaving his father. Oddly enough, it didn't surprise him. He was sad, but supportive. Two weeks later, Lilly flew to Michigan and told Dalton that she wanted a divorce. It was one of the hardest things she ever had to do. She felt responsible, like it was all her fault that the marriage was ending, and she had to keep reminding herself that it took two to get to this point, and of all the years of neglect from Dalton.

Dalton asked her not to go—to give him another chance—but it was too far beyond that. Lilly told him nothing would ever change. She did stay for several days to make sure he was going to be all right. To her surprise, the last day that she was there, Dalton called his friend George Ashton, who was a lawyer in Suttons Bay, and asked him to come out to the house. The three of them sat down, and Dalton explained the situation to George, and told him that Lilly was entitled to everything—all he wanted was this house, and enough money to get by for the time being.

Lilly was shocked and sad. She knew Dalton carried no ill will towards her, and that in his own tragic way he loved her. But Dalton was so submerged in his own world, and pain, he didn't know how to show her—or how too express his love. Lilly told Dalton she felt guilty walking away from him where she still loved him. She told him she felt that he desperately needed to be led from the darkness he'd created for himself, but she wasn't the one who could do it.

The situation took George off guard a little when Dalton called him, and that they were willing to work everything out without a fight was almost unheard of. George said he'd draw up some papers, and promised that the entire process wouldn't be long and drawn out. He was very sympathetic and kind to them both. Dalton got the house in Northport, and Lilly got the house in Yonkers. Everything else was split up reasonably. Dalton started drinking heavily, and Lilly stepped into her new life. She began to see Walter Covington, and within a year and a half from the divorce, she and Walter were married. Lilly sold the house in Yonkers, and she and Walter bought another home further north in Westchester County, in Tarrytown.

The bar was starting to fill up again, mostly with younger people. In fact, Dalton might have been the oldest guy in the bar. No one recognized him, and that was fine. He ordered another drink and looked at his watch. There was still another hour before the art opening was over.

"Mind if I sit here?" Dalton turned—it was Dan.

"Aren't you supposed to be somewhere?" Dalton asked.

"Right here, if that's all right with you."

"Be my guest," Dalton said. Dan sat down and waved at the bartender.

"Shows not over, is it?" Dalton asked.

"For the most part."

"Your mother?" Dalton asked.

"They left about a half an hour ago—headed back to Westchester."

"Julie?"

"Hell, I left her at the party," Dan said. "It'll be another hour before she realizes I'm gone." Dalton was surprised by his son's comment, and laughed out loud.

"She's quite a girl you got there."

"Yeah."

"You serious about this wedding?" Dalton said.

"I don't know—I guess so. Maybe."

"Your mother doesn't approve."

"I know," Dan said. "I could tell. She's a hard person to please."

"She's a good woman," Dalton said. "She just wants you to be happy—that's all."

"Wow—that wasn't the response I thought I'd get from you," Dan said.

"I've always loved your mother, Dan. It's not her fault we're not together any more."

"You drunk?" Dan asked, and Dalton gave him a sideways glance.

"Maybe a little, but that's okay.

Fifteen

Time seemed to stand still—and for a few hours Dalton and Dan sat there, not just as father and son, but equals—letting go of the past—the pain and all the unpleasant memories. Dalton didn't think about the fact that he was dying with cancer, or dwell on the notion that this was the first and probably last time that he and his son would share moments like this. No, if he dwelled on that, he'd be overwhelmed with regret. Instead, he wanted tonight to be a night to remember. He put everything aside, the cancer, the pain, the fact that he was an old man in this eternally youthful city, and he drank another beer and a shot of whiskey, and said to Dan, "Lets go have some fun."

Dan didn't feel much like painting the town red, and had things to do in the morning—but, after a beer and a shot of whiskey he too seemed to worry a little less about tomorrow. Dan idolized Dalton, and here, for probably the first time, they were on common ground, and together. It was a night out with his Dad, and there was no place he'd rather be than right there in that moment. So when Dalton said he wanted to go have some fun, Dan hesitated, but responded, "Absolutely."

They wandered back towards the East Village, occasionally stopping for another beer—here or there. Dalton told stories about the New York of the past, when he was young and full of fire to live, and love, and eager to write the next great American novel. After all these years, this was the first time Dan had ever really talked with his father. Dalton told stories Dan had never heard before, and he wondered how many more there were. It was like Dalton blossomed that night, and Dan saw him in his entirety for the first time.

Dalton wasn't just that sad lonely writer locked away in his den that Dan had known growing up—he was an entirely different person, one Dan had never known.

On the corner of Houston and Elizabeth Street, they wandered into *Tom & Jerry's*, a little bar with a high ceiling and an old worn wooden floor. It was crowded, but they found a table in the back where Dalton sat down, and Dan went to the bar to order their drinks. When he came back, he sat next to Dalton, shoulder to shoulder, looking out into the crowded bar.

"How is it," Dan said, "when you write it comes out so natural?"

"I'm honest," said Dalton.

"For me, I have to write, rewrite, and write it again" Dan said, "and often it still feels forced. I don't know how to get past that."

"Tell me this," Dalton said, "do you have a *muse*—a source of inspiration?"

"I don't know," Dan said, thinking about the question. "I guess I don't really. I suppose my agent would be a bad choice." Dalton laughed. "What about you—do you?"

"Mine has changed over time. Now-a-days I write for myself, but I think I'm writing to a younger version of myself. I think in a way I'm competing with him, showing him this old man can still write, create, and live as he could. Everything I write has a source of inspiration, someone who by merely thinking of them urges me on creatively, to keep writing, to keep being honest and to tell the story with as much truth as possible, whatever the story may be. Trying to write for everyone is a mistake, and it will bog you down. Find a *muse*, my boy."

"You didn't really answer the question, besides the younger version of yourself now-a-days, who was your *muse*?" Dan asked.

"I knew someone a long time ago," Dalton said. "She faded away. Even though she wasn't part of my life, I continued to think, write, and dream of her. Eventually, the thoughts and memories of her became an entity of their own, and that became my muse."

"Someone in your imagination, based on someone real?" Dan said.

"Yeah, exactly," said Dalton, "She's very real, but gone her own way, and I went mine."

"Someone you knew before mom?" Dan said.

"Sort of, she kind of came and went over the years. I was in love with her, and I thought she loved me. Life can get you all tangled up sometimes, and you can lose yourself in it. Your mother and I struggled a lot over the years... I should say I *struggled* while she tried to love me. Had I only seen your Mother then the way I see her today, I never would have let her go. I was caught up with myself and my *muse*, and I was blind to what was really happening with my life, and my family."

"Do I know this woman, the *muse*?" Dan asked.

"No," said Dalton.

"Does mom?"

"She knows her, not well. Hell, I don't even know her well anymore, my memories of her—the way she was years ago are all I have today, and the random details that emerge over time. You know, you hear this and that and sort of put the pieces together."

"Who is she?" asked Dan.

"Her name is Elizabeth Wharton," Dalton said. "She was married to my cousin Edward. Your Grandpa Gus's older brother, Ethan, married a young girl, Gertrude, and they only had one son, my cousin Edward. He was about three years older than me... born in 1933, I believe. Well, Uncle Ethan joined the navy in '41. A German submarine torpedoed the ship he was on, and, well, that just tore the ship apart, about one-third of the crew survived," Dalton said.

"They never found Ethan, and Gertrude had a nervous breakdown and spent the rest of her life in an institution, she passed away in '84 or '85, I can't remember.

Mom and Dad took cousin Edward in and raised him as their own." Dalton slid some cash across the table, "How bout getting us a couple more beers," he said, and Dan headed back to the bar.

The only other person Dalton had ever told this story to was Charlie, and even they never talk about it all any more. He also knew there would never be a better time to tell this story to Dan than right here, right now. Dan came back with two full pint glasses, and slid one in front of Dalton.

"How old was Edward when he moved in with you?" Dan asked.

"He was around eight years old," Dalton said. "When Edward was eighteen, he was drafted and went to Korea. He was over there for almost two years, was wounded and discharged. They sent him home.

While Edward was away, the Wharton's moved into a little place just out of town, Frank and Carolyn Wharton. They had two daughters, Mary and Elizabeth. Well, your Aunt Meg got to be good friends with them—they were always together. And I fell madly in love with Elizabeth.

In '56 Edward came home from Korea, and I went off to college. Well, it didn't take long for Edward to notice Elizabeth, she was so young and beautiful, everyone just loved her. Edward started to date her, and they got pretty serious.

I came home before Christmas, and Edward proposed to Elizabeth at the big holiday party on Christmas Eve, right there in front of everyone. I had no idea... it felt like someone shoved a knife into my chest. It was terrible. My young naive self always thought I'd come home from college and marry her.

I was in shock for the next few days, and then decided I had to tell her how I felt. On New Years Eve afternoon, we went for a walk along the shore towards the lighthouse, and I confessed my love for her, I told her I had always loved her and wanted to marry her. I begged her not to marry Edward. She cried, I cried, it was terrible. She wouldn't see me after that, and she and Edward were married in the spring of '57. I was twenty-one years old. That summer I dropped out of school and moved to New York, and that's where I met your mother. We were married in 1959.

A couple years passed, and I started getting letters from Elizabeth, your mother never thought anything of it because she was my cousin's wife, and I never let on how I had felt about her. So I started getting these letters, and she told me how Edward was drinking more, and having nightmares about the war. He was having post-traumatic stress, but none of us knew that then. He and Elizabeth were having all kinds of problems. I always wrote her back, and after a while, we had this entire relationship developing. We shared everything, and I looked forward to her letters. I think I liked the fact that she *needed* me.

Well, this went on for a long time. Later that year, I planned a trip home to see my Dad, your Grandpa Gus, and Elizabeth and I planned to meet. I remember every detail about that afternoon, our walk, and the way the sun shone through the trees and on her hair, the gulls, the rocks, and the smell of her perfume…

We walked around the lighthouse, and back to the house. We agreed to meet at an old motel just out of Traverse City on Highway 22. We were both terrified. She needed me, and I needed her. We were both running away from our lives. We made love, and I held her throughout the night, and for a moment I was at peace, and felt like we could handle all the rest as long as we were together. It was the most passionate, loving, and intimate moments I've ever experienced. When I woke up in the morning, she was gone."

Dalton took a long drink.

"Edward found all the letters I'd sent to Elizabeth, and confronted her with them. I guess it was terrible. He was drunk, and beat her up pretty bad, and she took off. Mom and Dad found out that Edward beat up Elizabeth, and Dad went to their house. Edward had hung himself in the garage. Dad was the one who found him."

"My god," Dan said. "I never knew that."

"No one talks about it."

"What happened to Elizabeth?"

"Well, after Edward's funeral she sold their house and left Northport. She just took off. I completely lost track of her for a while. I published my first novel, and then you were born. Your mom and I were happy; we moved into the place in Yonkers and everything seemed to be going so well, but I had some trouble publishing another novel, and started drinking too much. One afternoon you and your mom went into the city and I got drunk and started writing a letter to Elizabeth… Well, I never finished it, but your mom found it and it caused all kinds of trouble.

I really put your mother through hell, Dan," Dalton said. He took another long drink of the cold beer. The bar was filling up and getting loud.

"The craziest thing was, even though I never sent that letter, a few days later, I got a letter from Elizabeth, and she said many of the same things that I was feeling, but I never responded. I just couldn't, after what I'd been putting your mother through. I wanted things to work out.

Your Grandma Emily passed away, and then when your Grandpa Gus started getting sick, we spent a lot more time in Michigan, just helping him keep things up."

"I remember," Dan said.

"Well, your Grandpa's funeral was the next time I saw Elizabeth. I was so surprised to see her, and it was like no time had passed at all, and all those feeling I thought were gone resurfaced and it really twisted everything around for me. I was so confused and desperate. Nothing happened between us that time, but if it was up to me, it would have. I was still in love with her.

After the funeral I tried to stay in contact, but I heard very little from her. Your Mom, you, and I were splitting our time up between New York, and Michigan… and one day, while we were all at the house in Yonkers, I got a phone call from Elizabeth. She was in New York on vacation, and wanted to meet me at Grand Central Station, so I went. We met, and she told me she was engaged to be married."

Dalton and Dan both took a drink simultaneously.

"Well, this all took me by surprise. I didn't know what to say. I felt like she'd just ripped out my heart, again. I told her I was happy for her, and we had this awkward goodbye. I can still see her walking away that day.

Months later I got drunk and wrote her a long letter and mailed it this time, well, when I sobered up, I whished like hell I had never sent it. A few weeks later, I got a response, and she asked me not to contact her again. It really tore me up.

I pushed your mother away. I treated her so badly. Eventually she flew to Michigan and asked me for the divorce. How could I not give it to her after all I'd done," Dalton said. "Probably a little more information than you were wanting to know…"

"Well," Dan said, "No, not really. It explains a lot of things, Dad."

"I guess so," Dalton said, then took another drink.

"Is she still a *muse*?" Dan asked.

Dalton thought for a while, and took another drink.

"I still think about her," he said, "I wonder how she is, how her life turned out, but she's not my inspiration anymore. I suppose now-a-day's—even more so than a younger version of myself—God, or death is my *muse*. Everything I've written in the last few years has been very internal, struggles of man verses himself, verses the forces of nature, and time. Sometimes, though, I'm writing to your mother."

"Have you ever told her that?" Dan asked.

"I don't think I have to, she knows," Dalton said.

"She still reads all your work," Dan said.

"I know," said Dalton.

"What made you decide to kill your main character in this last novel?" Dan asked.

"I was resolving the character," Dalton said. "He'd been left unre-solved for so many years, through so many stories, I just felt it was time."

There was a long silence between them as they finished their beers.

"You ever talk to Angie anymore?" Dalton asked.

"No," Dan said quickly.

"I see her all the time, you know," Dalton said. "Helped her with her car this last week."

"I don't talk to her," Dan said, "and I don't think about her." Dan was being half honest, and knew that even if they sat there and talked about Angie all night, it wouldn't change things, and Dalton could see it was not a good subject to press.

They left *Tom & Jerry's* and made there way to the Bowery. Dalton loved this neighborhood, wandering these streets felt like he was walking back through time.

"I love this part of the city," Dalton said as they walked along. "The Lower East Side, Chinatown, Little Italy."

"You know they closed *CBGB's*," Dan said.

"I heard—but that place was a little after my time—I never was actually in there," Dalton said as they walked by on the opposite side of the street from where *CBGB's* use to be. "My time was earlier. When I was here, way back when, Dylan was playing in coffee shops and bars, and Ginsberg was wandering the streets."

"You ever meet any of those guys?" Dan asked.

"Saw Dylan back then, never met him though. I did meet Ginsberg—nice guy, a very sweet man—passionate about life, and writing. I was at *Chumley's* one night when Kerouac was there—he was pretty drunk, and so were the rest of us. Nothing really stands out from that night though—he was just there. I knew Jim Harrison pretty well, till he moved out west and we lost touch. Oh hell, there have been a lot of artist over the years I've ran with—been acquainted with—or just passed on the street." They walked along in silence for a bit and passed the *Bowery Poetry Club*. Dalton stopped when he saw the picture of Kerouac in the window. "Hey, what's this place?"

"Another bar," Dan said, "shall we?" He led the way inside. There were some book shelves off to the left—then the bar was back to the right. Way in the back was a stage where a guy was setting up a microphone and adjusting lights.

"Hey," Dalton said, "this looks like the place to be—their going to have a show or something." They made their way back to the bar and took off their coats. Dalton nodded to the bartender, and he came and took their orders and brought them some beers.

"I saw you had a notebook out earlier—were you writing tonight?" Dan asked.

"No. Just remembering," Dalton said. "Always keep a journal—I always have, and it's invaluable. As time passes, you forget, or your memories are distorted. A journal is the best way to access the past—to go back in time."

"Where were you tonight?" Dan asked.

"All over—trying to find some meaning and understanding—trying to resolve a few things."

"You sound like your going to die," Dan laughed.

"We're all gonna die, son," Dalton said. He thought about the cancer, and telling Dan—but this wasn't the time. They both sat there sipping their beers without speaking. They were both feeling like they knew something no one else knew—a quiet understanding of themselves—of each other; and here they were in this sad, lonely world—together.

"Dad, what do you think it's all about?"

"What's that?"

"Life—all this. You've been through it all—a successful writer, husband, brother, father—what meaning have you come to?"

Dalton took another drink and thought for a moment.

"We're all doing the best we can, and I think that's a big part of the story. Everyone's no better or worse, we're all just going through the motions, and hopefully it'll lead to something better—or as good—more fulfilling, a better life, possibly a better world. Everyone has problems. Everyone has dreams, needs. We all wake up day after day wondering what were going to do. Where we're going—happy, sad, wondering, 'am I living life fully?' We all have troubles. But if you keep moving, you work through them and move on. Everything is temporary. Everything is at our fingertips. Life is what you make of it, and I really think, we're all just doing the best we can."

They both took another drink.

"Dad," Dan said, "the things I want the most I'm not doing—I find it hard to be creative, to have a stable relationship. I'm constantly looking for the time and energy to become something other than what I am. Julie says I'm self-absorbed."

"So what is the question?" Dalton asked.

"How the hell did you find time to do it all?"

"Well—I did a lot, but it wasn't all successfully."

"I don't know about that," Dan said, thinking about his father's fame, published novels, and bank account.

"I sacrificed my family Dan," Dalton said.

"There's no such thing as a perfect family, Dad."

"I know, but I could've tried harder. My wife left me. This is the first time you and I've ever had a night quite like this. I just don't feel like I gave it my all."

"But you were focused on your writing, and because of that, you afforded us a lot of opportunities."

"I was focused on myself," Dalton said, staring down into his drink. "I think the most important thing is love, attention, and praise from your parents—to instill the belief that you can grow up and do anything. You know, your grandfather—he was a good man—but he never understood me. He never gave us praise. He never told me he loved me. I know he did, it was kind of understood. It was so hard for him to express any emotion. My mother did all that for him, and it wasn't till she died that my Dad started to open up a little. He never approved of what I did, why I wouldn't just learn a trade—or get a job at a factory in Detroit, or something, like all the other guys my age. My cousin Edward, he joined the military, served his time. He came home and did everything right. Dad was proud of him. He'd say—look at Edward—why can't you be more like him.

I guess what I'm getting at is, I never got the praise and attention from him I needed, and I always swore if I ever had a kid I wouldn't do that to him—and now here I am all these years later, damn near in the same boat. I was the same man—and I wasn't a very good father."

"Look Dad—look at me, here in New York City, trying to make a go of it—if it wasn't for your influence, who knows where I might be today, what I may be doing."

"You've done good Dan. I'm proud of you."

A new bartender started her shift. She came out and took their order. When she brought their beers back, she hesitated and grinned, "Might you be Dalton Jones?" she asked. The men looked at one another and Dan smiled. For Dan these moments were always bitter sweet; he longed for his fathers notoriety and fame. There was a twinge of jealousy, but it faded quickly.

"Yes, I am," Dalton said humbly.

She stuck out her hand and shook his.

"Wow. What an honor, Sir. I've read everything you've ever written. This last novel—*amazing*," she said. She was animated and cute, and very young. "It was by far my favorite, so far."

"Thank you," Dalton said. "This is my son, Dan," shifting the conversation and attention elsewhere. Dan shook her hand and smiled.

"Oh my-gosh, I didn't know you had a son," she blushed. "He's cute," she said to Dalton. "You look just like your dad," she grinned to

Dan. They all smiled. Dalton reached for his wallet, but she refused.

"These are on me, boys," she said, and backed away.

Dalton looked over to Dan, "Well, at least I gave you my good looks," and smiled.

"I'll drink to that," Dan laughed, and they lifted their glasses and took a drink.

"So what's happening with that book of yours?" Dalton asked.

"Oh, yeah," Dan said, not wanting to tell him that the book was rejected again. He didn't want sympathy, or advice, he just wanted to forget about it—the same as Dalton wanted to forget about his cancer. "I haven't heard anything back yet," he lied. "You know how these things can drag on."

"Oh yes I do," Dalton said. "Hang in there, I'm sure they will love it. I can't wait to read it."

Hearing Dalton say that felt like getting a load of cinder blocks dropped on him. Dan never thought about his father sitting and reading his book—only the publishers, agents, and friends. Dan had a moment of panic—what would his dad think? Would he like it at all? Hell, maybe he'd hate it—and would he be able to tell Dan the truth? He wondered if he should have had Dalton read it before he ever started submitting it to the publisher.

"Maybe I can read an advanced copy," Dalton said, "I'm not getting any younger you know."

"Yeah, sure—I'll get another copy printed and send it to you. It may still need some revisions."

"Oh absolutely. I've had to rewrite several novels, nothings final till it's printed."

"You had to rewrite?"

"Oh, hell yes. You think they loved everything I ever wrote?" Dalton laughed. "Some of the most frustrating times of my life, to work on something for months..." Dalton said.

"Or years," Dan said.

"...Or years, and have someone say "no good," and send it back to you all marked up. That's just a terrible feeling."

"I know," Dan said, understanding completely what he was talking about.

"But then there's times when they love the first draft, I guess those times make it all worthwhile," Dalton said. Dan smiled, wishing he knew what that felt like. They drank in silence for a moment or two, and the young bartender came back over to them.

"I don't know if you're interested or not, but were going to have a poetry reading in here in about fifteen minutes—we'd love it if you'd read something."

At first, Dalton's initial reaction was "no way," and then he thought about what he'd have done thirty years ago to an offer like that—he knew he would've done it.

Dan sat there watching Dalton's expression, wondering what his response was going to be.

"For another round of drinks, I'll read something," Dalton said. She laughed out loud and said it was a deal.

"Well, that surprises me!" Dan said as the young bartender ran to tell the man who was setting up the microphone.

"It's a special night," Dalton said. "Full of surprises." Dalton pulled his old journal out of his pocket and flipped through the pages. He knew there was something in there he could read, and turned to the late night drunken poem he sent to Elizabeth all those years ago, *Another Dream of You*. He paused a long moment, re-read the first few lines, and knew this was it. He dog-eared the page and laid the old journal on the bar.

"Find something?" Dan asked.

"Found it."

Sixteen

The lights in the back of the bar were dimmed, and the spotlight was intense. The guy running the poetry reading motioned for the young bartender to come up to the stage. She went to the microphone and seemed a little nervous, squinting her eyes in the bright light.

"Hi everyone," she said. There was a low murmur from the crowd, people were still finding their seats, and getting drinks. "We have a special treat for you tonight. May I present to you... the author, Mr. Dalton Jones."

The crowd went to a disbelieving hush when Dalton turned from the bar and started for the stage. There was a lite applause as he walked through the crowd, with drink and notebook in hand. He stepped up onto the stage, to the microphone. Looking over to the young bartender, he asked, "Can I get a stool, I'm pretty old and a little drunk."

The crowd laughed nervously, anxiously anticipating what was next. The young bartender brought Dalton a stool, he finished his drink and set it on the edge of the stage. He sat down on the stool, positioned the microphone, and cleared his throat.

"It's good to be back in the Bowery," Dalton said, looking out at the crowd. Another lite applause "I'm a little unprepared, wasn't expecting to do this tonight, but sometimes life presents you with opportunities and you have to seize them—*carpe diem*, right?" He opened his journal and cleared his throat again.

Dan, still watching from the back, thought how at ease his father seemed in front of the crowd, and he wondered if that came with age and maturity, or the booze.

"I'm not going to read anything from my new novel," Dalton said. "I don't have it with me. But, I'd like to read something I wrote a long time ago when I lived here in New York. It's unpublished, and the working title is *Another Dream of You*." Dalton looked back towards the bar, squinting his eyes into the light, "I'd love another beer if you wouldn't mind." The bartender nodded. "Put it on my son's tab," Dalton said with a grin. "Ladies and gentlemen, that's my son back there at the bar, Dan Jones—stand up Dan—a very talented young man." Dan stood up, slightly embarrassed, and the crowd applauded him. Dalton smiled, and thanked the young bartender for the beer she handed him. He took a sip and set it on the stage next to him. As he bent over, he hurt real bad in his lower back; it was the first time in a few hours that the pain was that intense, and it reminded him that he was dying, and that these were perhaps some of the final scenes to his story. He looked out across the crowd of unknown faces, and thought this would be the perfect ending if this were all a novel.

"*Another Dream of You*," Dalton said again, and cleared his throat. The crowd grew silent.

"*Cold nights in the east Village, wandering the Bowery, Tompkins Square. In flashing faces of passing subway trains, I think I see you. I imagine you in the green grass of Union Square, or on the corner of Third and St. Marks. In my mind I act out our meeting, our embrace, soft-spoken words, our love making on soft sheets in secret city hideaway. You came to me, I didn't ask for you, or want you, but when I finally saw you I was awestruck, and there was nothing I could do but stare. Knowing I couldn't touch you made you that much more desirable. I dreamt of you, and in my thoughts we became one, your light and mine were interchanging, lit from the same flame, burning.*

I hear less from you these days, awkward letters and time separate us. It's been over a year and I have no idea where you are. I think back to another time, through aged eyes I saw you then, you were so young. Who was I to pluck your petals of youth to satisfy my lustful desires, tainting the very thing I craved. Even now as I hold you in my secret

dream desire, I remember the way you held me, what seemed an eternity was only a night, a few hours. You welcomed my touch, leading my
hands against your
longing skin, your lips were soft and sweet. Somehow..."

Dalton's voice cracked, and trailed off briefly.

"*Somehow I've remained consumed by you all this time. Even
today, my desire for you lingers like the hot embers of yesterday's fire. I
imagine you feeling that which burns through me inside of you.*

*The last time I saw you something exploded deep within. It had
been years, I'd claimed that we were just friends—but I hadn't seen you.
We were drawn together, looking through one another, never seeing the
other wholly in this new light. Finding you again, I knew we were lovers.
As I embraced you—holding your body, I was longing to push my way
inside, to protect you, or be protected. But I was weak, and lost, leaving
me only to yearn for you as you drifted away into darkness.*

*Drunk and alone, I find my way to the street, the building, the
lonely room, unable to sleep on this cold mattress, I long to dream
of you. I thought for a moment I heard you call out to me, but it was
nothing more than the drunken chorus of fate. I drift off into dream,
where you sat fully clothed on my naked lap and cried. I awake in this
dreary, dim lit room, where I can still hear your voice, and taste salty
tears on my lips.*"

There was a moment of silence, and then the crowd began to
applaud, and continued to applaud, and then some began to stand
up and they gave him a rowdy drunken New York City ovation. Dalton was humbled by this, so grateful. He stood up, graciously took
a bow, and left the stage. As he stepped from the spotlight, he again
thought that if this were a novel, this would be the perfect ending.

*Leelanau State Park campgrounds, looking
out towards Grand Traverse Bay.*

Northern point of Leelanau Peninsula,
along the Lake Michigan shoreline.

PART II

Seventeen

Dalton left New York City the next morning, and was home to Northport that evening. The house was dark as he came through the back door, and there was old Sam sitting on the kitchen table. Dalton set his bags down, he was hurting badly this evening—he turned up the furnace, and scratched Sam on top of the head. He opened the blinds in the living room and started a fire in the fireplace—getting down to his knees was hard, and he had to use the wall for support to get back up again. The pain was getting worse. He shuffled around the house for a while and decided to call Aaron Mackenzie—the office was closed, so he called him at home.

"Aaron," Dalton said, "Yes, I'm home. It's getting worse. Can you give me something more for the pain?"

Dalton stood there in the empty house, listening, nodding his head. "I understand," he said. "Can I come in the morning? Okay… Thank you. I'll see you in the morning." He hung up the phone and stared out the window. Dalton knew where this was all heading, and was scared—not of the thought of death—but of how bad this pain might get before the end. He was glad that he had this last weekend with Dan, even though it was hard on him physically, he knew there wouldn't be another one like it.

Dalton poured warm whiskey into a glass and sat in his easy chair by the fire. The rest of the house was dark. Sam jumped into Dalton's lap. The blinds were still open and the moonlight silhouetted the pines surrounding the house. The sky was clear and the stars were bright. Dalton's thoughts returned to Dan, and he hoped things would start to take off for him. Dan needed something big to happen to set him assail, that first big break. It's never the going, it's the getting started that takes so damn long. To Dalton, it seemed like just yesterday his career took off, and now it was almost over. All those years of struggle and worry, and the stress of making the right moves, the right agents, the right books, and words—and how little any of it seemed to matter now.

Dalton listened to the fire crackle and watched through the picture window as the big pine bows rocked back and forth in the breeze. How quickly life slips away he thought, and closed his eyes and fell asleep.

Eighteen

Meg drove Charlie and Hank, the Australian shepherd, over to Dalton's place out on Cathead Bay. They hadn't heard from Dalton since he got back from New York and decided it was time to drop in on him. They saw his old pickup when they pulled into the driveway. As they got out of the car Hank jumped over Charlie and was the first to the house. Meg knocked on the back door, but there was no answer. The door was unlocked so they went inside. The house was dark and quiet.

"He's here," Meg said, "his coat and hat are hanging up."

"He's probably asleep," Charlie said. "You start lunch, and I'll go look upstairs." Meg went to work unpacking the hot lunch she'd brought from home, and Charlie picked up an empty coffee cup setting on the counter top, inspected it to see if it was clean, filled it with ice from the freezer and went up stairs. When he got to the top of the stairs he saw Sam stick his head out of the bathroom like a watchdog. Charlie tapped on the bathroom door lightly. Dalton sat up in the tub…

"Whose there?" Dalton said.

"It's me," Charlie said as he walked into the bathroom. Dalton leaned back into the deep tub of hot water. Sam was back on the stool next to Dalton, and Charlie sat down on the lid closed toilet. He reached for the half full fifth of whiskey Dalton had been sipping from. "You mind?" Charlie asked as he poured warm whiskey over the ice in his coffee cup.

"What if I did?" Dalton said.

"I just can't shake this cough," Charlie said.

"You've had that cough ever since I've known you." Dalton said. Charlie took a drink.

"You know it's the cigarettes—there going to kill you." Dalton said.

"Says the dying man," Charlie said. "Besides, I don't smoke anymore," as he took the pack of cigarettes out of his shirt pocket and put them in his jackets inside pocket. "How was the big apple?"

"Fine," Dalton said.

"Lilly?"

"Fine,"

"Dan?" Charlie asked.

"He's good," Dalton said. Charlie was taking another drink when Hank wandered into the bathroom, Charlie told him to sit and Hank laid down next to the tub.

"This room is getting a little small," Dalton said.

"Snowed while you were gone," Charlie said. "Was real cold."

"That's a surprise," Dalton said.

"Why didn't we all move someplace warm after Gus died?" Charlie said.

"Didn't want to," Dalton said. Hank scratched himself and the tags on his collar clinked together.

"I always thought Florida, or Arizona would have been nice," Charlie said.

"Too hot," Dalton said. Hank stood up and licked Dalton's wet knee. "Alright! Charlie can you get him the hell out of here!" Charlie laughed, and Meg swung open the bathroom door and stepped in.

"Lunch is ready," She said.

"God damn it!" Dalton yelled trying to cover himself, and Charlie continued to laugh. "You people have crossed the line! What ever happened to a little privacy!" Charlie still laughing picked up the bottle of whiskey and stood up redirecting Meg and Hank out of the bathroom.

"What's the matter with him?" Meg asked, confused.

"See you downstairs for lunch," Charlie said, still laughing.

Dalton looked over at Sam still sitting on the stool with one ear cocked.

"That means you too!" Dalton growled, and Sam hopped off the stool and left the bathroom.

When Dalton came downstairs Meg was flitting about the kitchen, and Charlie was sitting at the table nursing his drink with Hank at his feet. By the smell of things Dalton figured it was home-made chicken soup.

"Sit down," Meg said when she saw Dalton, and served him a bowl of hot soup, then one for Charlie. She went back to the stove and put the buttered bread with cheese in the hot frying pan, it sizzled, and she grilled each side, cut it in half with the spatula, and served the grilled cheese to the men. "You want coffee?" Meg asked Dalton.

"No, thank you," he said. "Sit down Meg, you better eat too."

"Oh, I ate earlier," she said as she sat down at the end of the table, took a sip of her cold coffee, got back up and poured herself, and Dalton a cup. She set it in front of him, and even though he said he didn't want any, he drank it. Meg set hers down at the end of the table, and as the men ate their lunch she went to wiping down the counter-tops.

"So how was the big art show?" Meg asked as she put a new bag in the trash-can.

"It was interesting," Dalton said. "Lots of people."

"Did you get a chance to talk to Dan?" Meg asked as her eyes welled up with tears, "to tell him… ?" Dalton hated to see her cry.

"I didn't," he said. "There never seemed to be a good time." Meg nodded her head and a tear rolled down her cheek.

"Have you made it back to the doctor for any more follow up?" Meg asked.

"I did, this morning actually," Dalton said, and set his spoon down. "I need to talk to you two about that." Meg stopped what she was doing, and Charlie glanced up over his glasses as he slurped his soup. "I've decided that I'm not going to do the chemo and the therapy," Dalton said. Charlie sat straight up in his chair, but didn't say a thing.

"Oh Dalton!" Meg cried.

"Now god damn it!" Dalton said frustrated, scared, "the cancer is bad Meg—real bad, and the treatment will only prolong the inevitable—and to tell you the truth, the treatment sounds almost as bad as the cancer. I don't want to go through what Daddy went through—you remember how horrible that was?" Meg nodded her head, she couldn't speak, and turned towards the sink with her head in her hands, and sobbed. Dalton looked to Charlie as if he should do something, but Charlie just starred back at him blankly. Dalton got up and went to Meg and embraced her, and she wept on his shoulder.

"God damn it," Dalton whispered, "I'm the one dying here."

They stood there for a long time in a tight embrace. Charlie sat at the table starring out the window. This was the first moment all three of them fully understood that Dalton was going to die.

Nineteen

Dan sat straddling the toilet, facing out the open bathroom window of his East Village apartment. He took a long drag off a cigarette, and blew smoke out the window. This was where he smoked so Julie wouldn't come home and get mad. He didn't know why he cared, it was his apartment. It was just easier this way, and he wouldn't have to listen to her complain. He put out the cigarette, and lit another one. He was thinking about what his agent said about writing a book about Dalton. Hell, all kinds of people have wrote books about their famous parents—but it was ultimately for their parents.

This life as a starving artist wasn't working out too well. Living in New York City the money goes fast—and Dan was running out of cash and was having to ask Dalton for money more frequently. He knew he should've asked him for more while he was there, but it just never felt like the right time. Dan knew Dalton would always help him in the end, but usually there was a long uncomfortable silence before he'd write the check.

Lilly would always tell Dan not to feel bad about asking for help from his father, she'd say for all the time he missed when you were a kid, the least he could do is help a little now. When she said it like that it made it a little easier, except not this last visit. This was the first time Dan felt like Dalton looked at him as an equal, and Dan didn't want that to end because of "the money conversation."

Besides an occasional allowance, Dalton paid for Dan's East Village apartment. Dan had been handed almost everything in life, and never had to work for what he needed. Everything always came easy;

everything except this book he'd wrote. This was one of the first times in his life he's dealt with this kind of rejection, and there was nothing his parents could do to help, this was entirely on Dan's shoulders.

He finished the cigarette while watching a plane fly out over the east river. He could hear someone yelling from the street, taxi's honking and that smell of curry from the Indian restaurant below. He had to figure out what to do next. Something that would make his father proud.

Twenty

4:36 A.M. Dalton woke up and sat on the edge of his bed, feet touching the cold floor. He walked to the bathroom to urinate—it only trickled and burned. He drew a hot bath and remembered the whiskey was down stairs. He stumbled down though the dark, to the kitchen, past the big chair in the living room and the kitchen table. Dalton picked up the half empty bottle of whiskey and went back upstairs.

Steam came off the bath water, and when he stepped into the tub, the water burned his feet and calves. He lowered himself down, leaned back slowly, and exhaled. His god damn back ached something terrible. He took a long pull from the bottle, and the warm whiskey went down easy, then he set the bottle down and closed his eyes.

This cancer was damn inconvenient he thought. At this rate without any treatment it wouldn't be long before it was all over. His thoughts took him to a place where everything was black and still, and he contemplated the end.

After the bath Dalton got dressed, fed the cat, made coffee—only to pour it out, and drank more whiskey. He sat at the table and tried to write, but it wasn't happening. He could write anywhere, but when it didn't flow freely he usually needed to change locations.

Around noon he finished the bottle, and put on his coat, hat, and gloves, and headed to town to the Grandview. He could always write there, it had good light in the afternoon and was relatively quiet.

Dalton could tell he was getting more tired than usual, and tried to fight it. There was still so much to do, and this god damn cancer was stealing his time faster than he'd expected.

He parked in a big open spot around the corner from the Grand-view. He didn't bother locking the doors when he climbed out of the truck, and stepped over the pile of dirty snow along the curb from where the sidewalk had recently been shoveled. There was ice so he walked slowly, not wanting to fall. He made it almost to the front door when he heard a familiar voice call out,

"Pretty early for a drink." Dalton stopped and turned around, it was Angie and Billy coming around the corner towards him.

"What's that?" Dalton said, and Angie smiled.

"I said—pretty early for a drink."

"Oh," Dalton responded. Most people he would have either ignored, or grinned and went on, but with Angie for some reason he was compelled to explain himself. "Well," he held up his journal, "I write in here sometimes. Good light." Angie smiled.

"Don't you have a special place to write at home?" She asked.

"I used to—but my wife took the desk," Dalton said. Angie wasn't sure if he was serious or joking. Dalton looked at Billy who was stand-ing close to his mother. "How are you Billy?"

"Fine," Billy said.

"Good," Dalton said, and smiled. There was a long silence. "Car running all right?"

"Oh, yeah," Angie said. "Starts right up."

"What are you writing?" Billy asked.

"Well, I'm writing in my journal—I guess just about stuff I've been thinking about."

"What sort of things?" Billy asked.

"Okay Billy," Angie said putting her hand on Billy shoulder. "It's cold out here and we have to get home, we'll see you later Dalton," Angie said, and smiled.

"Okay," Dalton said, "see you later."

As they walked away Billy turned and waved goodbye, leaving Dalton feeling this vast wave of loneliness. He shook it off quickly and went inside the Grandview where it was warm and smelled like beer and peanuts. Eugene was behind the bar wiping glasses and shelving them.

"Morning Eugene," Dalton said as he stomped his snowy boots on the floor mat.

"Whiskey?" Eugene asked with a cigarette hanging from his lips. Dalton nodded. "Writing?"

"Yep," Dalton said, and walked to the back of the bar and took his usual seat. Eugene brought him his drink and set it on the wooden table.

"Colder than piss out there," Eugene said.

"Hadn't noticed," Dalton said.

Eugene grunted and walked back to the bar. For the next four hours Dalton wrote, and sipped whiskey.

About 4:20 P.M. he looked up at the clock and realized he'd been awake for about twelve hours and the whiskey had pretty well numbed him up.

The front door swung open and Charlie walked in with Hank at his heels. Charlie semi-waved when Dalton glanced up from his journal. Charlie took off his coat and took a seat at the bar—Hank laid down at his feet.

"Afternoon Mr. Wixson!" Charlie said to Eugene. Eugene grinned, and ashed his cigarette.

"What's new Charles?" Eugene asked.

"It's colder than piss out there—besides that, nothing." Eugene served Charlie a beer and a shot of whiskey. Charlie ate some peanuts from the dish on the bar, and looked over his shoulder to Dalton. "How long has he been in here?"

"Three, maybe four hours," Eugene said. Charlie nodded and sipped his beer as Eugene wiped off the bar again.

"You hear Jones ran Paul Harper out of town?" said Eugene

"What?" Charlie said.

"That's what I heard from Bob Conrad. Said Dalton drove right up into Angie Bartlett's front yard, almost ran over Bob's rhododendron bushes. Bob's wife saw Dalton toss Harper off the front porch."

"Dalton hasn't said a thing about it," Charlie said, and looked over his shoulder to Dalton, who was still scribbling away in his notebook.

"According to Mike Preston's wife, Harper's shacking up with some gal down in Maple City. That's all I've heard," Eugene said, and lit a cigarette. "I didn't ask Dalton about it. I didn't want to pry for information—I'm not much for gossip." Charlie nodded again and sipped his beer. He turned and stared out the front window as the wind blew and the drifting snow swirled down the street. He figured the people out walking were cursing this cold Michigan winter.

"Eugene," Charlie said, "your older than I am—what the hell is the meaning of it all? What do you know for sure?"

Eugene stopped what he was doing, and the afternoon light lit one side of his grim, weathered face.

"Nothing," said Eugene.

"Nothing?" said Charlie surprised.

"Absolutely nothing," Eugene said.

"Not quite the uplifting message of hope that I was looking for," Charlie said.

"Chuck—I've lived a long time. Seen a lot of things and nothing is for certain, everything changes. Time seems to alter things, my parents, brothers, wife, son, all dead. My favorite dog is dead. I pay more for gas today than I ever have, I take pills everyday that cost a fortune to keep me alive, and for what? This old bar is falling apart, and besides my Granddaughter Adley, I can't find any kids anymore who want to work—work the way I worked when I came back from the war. I've lost my hair, my hearing, and can barely get a hard-on. I look forward to a healthy shit and a good nights sleep." Eugene took another long drag off his cigarette and exhaled. "It's nice to hear from my other grandkids, but I don't know them." Eugene paused again and looked out the front window. The sun filled his old face with light. "I have a lot of thoughts and feelings about things, but I don't know anything for sure."

"I guess you know that much," Charlie said.

"I guess I do," said Eugene.

"I suppose right there is the question of our lives," Charlie said, "and answer."

Eugene nodded in agreement.

Charlie held up the shot of whisky, "to the problems of life."

"Here, here," Eugene said. He poured Charlie another whiskey, and set it in front of him. About then a couple came into the bar. Eugene cleared his throat, put out his cigarette and went over to them to take their order.

Charlie sat there in silence for a while, life had been weighing on him heavily since yesterday afternoon at Dalton's place. He was trying to get his arm around the thought that Dalton was going to die. It all seemed like a bad dream. He turned on his stool and faced Dalton who was busy writing, and sipping whiskey. Charlie picked up his beer and jacket and walked back to Dalton's table, Hank followed.

"Mind if I sit down?" said Charlie.

"Go ahead," Dalton said still writing. Charlie hung his coat on the back of the chair and sat across the table from Dalton, and sipped his beer until Dalton finished writing. Dalton closed the journal, set the pen on the table, and looked up at Charlie—they were both a little drunk.

"Do you believe in God?" Charlie asked.

"Yes," Dalton said.

"How do you know?"

"I don't know—just got a feeling, I guess."

"How do you feel about dying?"

"*Jesus* Charlie!" Dalton said.

"Really—how do you feel?" Dalton squirmed.

"I ain't ready," Dalton said.

"To answer—or for death?" asked Charlie.

"Neither," Dalton said.

"My world renowned brother-in-law, the writer, who has wrote thousands and thousands of words can't think of a god damn thing to say!" Charlie said. Dalton grimaced.

"What the hell am I supposed to say?" said Dalton. "I'm going to die. I don't know how much time I have left. How the hell would you feel if you were me? What would you do?"

"Oh hell," Charlie said, "the first thing I'd do is finish this drink, then I'd go home and tell your sister how much I love her."

"Well, those are both good things," said Dalton.

"Do you ever wonder what it's all been about?" Charlie asked, then sipped his beer.

"Everyday," said Dalton.

"I think about that a lot," Charlie continued. "You have a son, you've had a family, wrote books, traveled the world. A hundred years from now if people want to know who Dalton Jones was, all they will have to do is look around a little, but me… I've left no legacy. Well, besides my bar tab here!" They both laughed a little and sipped their drinks.

"I've got nothing to leave behind. If Meg and I would've been younger maybe we could've had kids," Charlie said looking off in the distance. His eyes teared up a little as he leaned back in his chair.

"I think about when I was a kid a lot, you know, both my brothers have passed on, but I think of them like they're still here, talking to me sometimes. I think about when we were kids and…" Charlie got all choked up and took a drink.

"Especially this time of the year, so close to the holidays." He leaned forward, elbows on the table. "I love Meg, you know that, but I was the happiest when I was a kid, with my brothers, my mother and father." Charlie wiped a real tear from the corner of his eye with his big fingers. Neither of them talked for a moment, and Dalton stared down at the top of the table, giving Charlie a moment.

A few more people came in and sat down at a table. Eugene put a few quarters into the jukebox. Sinatra's version of *I'll be home for Christmas* started to play, and Charlie took a deep breath and lifted his glass to Dalton…

"To family," he said, and they drank.

"Are you still in love with Elizabeth?" Charlie asked. Dalton was taken off guard, but appreciated the fact that Charlie didn't mince words—if he thought it—he usually said it.

"No, I don't think so," Dalton said, "I think I've been in love with a memory—a few moments I've lived over and over. I was in love with her once—but not anymore."

"Did you go listen to her speak the other night?"

"I did," Dalton said.

"I thought you did," Charlie said. He wasn't surprised. "Did you talk to her?"

"No," Dalton said. "I left right afterwards."

"Why not?" Charlie asked.

"Oh—I don't know," Dalton said as he leaned back in his chair. "I got scared." Charlie laughed out loud.

"Scared of what?" Charlie asked. Dalton was staring at the top of the table again—staring hard into his drink.

"Scared that I'd talk to her, look into her eyes and regret the last forty years of my life."

"Oh," Charlie said.

"You know, I don't think about her, but there, in the past when we've crossed paths, I just become consumed by her. I don't have any control over it, it's like getting caught in a storm.

The other day after I read that article Meg gave me, it was all I could think about. I must have read that paper twenty times, so there I was getting caught up in the storm again after all this time. I had to go listen to her speak. You know, she was older, but seemed the same. I wanted to run down there and embrace her, and tell her so many things about my life, and death—but I couldn't, I got scared, and I left."

"Do you wish you would've talked to her now?"

"I don't know. No. Yes. Yes, I do. I wish I could have told her I was going to die, and I hope she's had a happy life."

"You want resolution," Charlie said.

"Yes, I want resolution with a lot of things—I've left a lot of loose ends over the years."

"Why don't you write her a letter?" Charlie said.

"I don't have her address," Dalton said, looking down again.

"Meg's got it," Charlie said.

"Oh," Dalton said, and took a drink.

"How was it seeing Lilly?" Charlie asked.

"It was fine," Dalton smiled a little. "She looks great, seems happy."

"How do you feel when you see her?" Charlie asked.

"She's my wife!" Dalton said. "I love her—I've never stopped loving her. I never wanted her to leave, but it hurt to see her so unhappy. I guess I loved her so much, and hurt her so much… I had to set her free. I never wanted her to be unhappy."

Outside it started snowing again and the streetlights came on.

"To Lilly," Charlie said lifting his glass.

"To Lilly," Dalton said, and they drank.

The bar was starting to fill up. Eugene was popping corn, and pouring beer. His granddaughter Adley showed up and got behind the bar to help, and Eugene took that as an opportunity to sit down and smoke a cigarette.

"Have I ever told you I love you?" Charlie said, tearing up again.

"Oh *Jesus*!" Dalton said, "Only every other time we sit together in here, quit acting like an old lady! Do you want another beer?"

Charlie laughed, finished his drink and stood up.

"Actually, no—well—would I like another—yes—am I going to have another—no." He put on his coat and hat.

"Need a ride home?"

"No. Hank and I are going to walk, it's a nice night."

"Cold," Dalton said.

"It's December in Michigan," Charlie said, and Dalton agreed.

"Good night my friend," Charlie said. He turned and walked towards the door, with Hank following close behind. Charlie waved to Eugene. Bing Crosby sang *White Christmas* on the jukebox, the bell on the door chimed as the door opened and closed, and Dalton watched Charlie step out, and away into the falling snow.

Dalton didn't feel like writing anymore and moved up to the bar. Adley was busy, and Eugene was sitting again, smoking another cigarette.

"What did you solve today Mr. Jones?" Eugene asked.

"World peace," Dalton said.

"What will you have?" Eugene asked.

"One more," Dalton said holding up his whiskey glass.

"You'd have been better off buying the entire bottle this morning," Eugene said. Dalton didn't respond. "You look tired Jones."

"That hurts coming from a ninety-year-old," said Dalton.

Eugene smiled, while pouring whiskey into Dalton's glass.

Twenty-one

Meg stood at the sink washing dishes and watching out the window for Charlie, he was late again. She expected him to call at any time from the Grandview—that was the usual routine. If it bothered her, she never said. She'd made beef stew for dinner and it would keep.

It was dark and cold, and a blanket of fresh snow covered the peninsula. Everything seemed still, even inside the house. Meg glanced around the kitchen, everything was clean and in it's place.

She finished the dishes and drained the soapy water from the sink, dried her hands on her apron, and caught herself humming a song her mother use to sing, and it made her smile. She wiped off the table again and was lighting a candle when she heard a noise from the back door, it sounded like Hank pawing at the screen. She turned the back porch light on for Charlie and started to set the table for his supper. Hank pawed at the screen door again. She figured Charlie had drank so much he couldn't get the key in the door, so she went to the back door and pulled the shade, but didn't see Charlie. She opened the door and there was Hank sitting on the back porch whining. When Meg opened the door all the way, Hank didn't come in, he stood up and paced back and forth while looking down the dark driveway, then back to Meg.

"Charlie?" Meg called out. "Where is he, Hank?" Hank whined again, and started down the driveway, then stopped and looked back for Meg. She got scared—Hank never left Charlie's side. She slipped on a pair of Charlie's old boots, and grabbed a flashlight and jacket.

It was cold. Her breath filled the air as she stepped off the porch into the night.

Meg followed Hank down to the end of the driveway, shining the flashlight towards him.

"Charlie?" she called out. Then Meg saw him. He was laying there on his side, in the snow bank. "Charlie!" Meg screamed.

As she ran to him, she lost a boot in the snow. "Oh no, Charlie!" she cried, but he wasn't moving or responding.

She knelt down beside him, "Oh god! Oh Charlie!"

Twenty-two

As Dalton unlocked the back door of the house, the telephone rang. The answering machine picked up the call it was Meg—she was sobbing—he couldn't make out what she was saying. Dalton rushed to the phone.

"Meg," Dalton said, "What's the matter?" She continued to cry.

"Oh god, Dalton," was all she said.

"Are you all right?" He asked beginning to panic, "Is it Charlie?"

"Yes," Meg said, "Charlie's gone."

"Where'd he go?"

"No, no," Meg cried. "He's had a heart attack, Dalton. He died." Dalton went numb all over. This couldn't be happening—this could not be happening.

"I'll be right there," he said and hung up the phone. He leaned against the wall, and was completely sober in seconds. He could feel the pain in his bones again—he looked at the whiskey bottle on the counter top and walked by it as he went out the back door to the truck.

He drove fast, back towards town, to Meg and Charlie's house. When he got there he saw the boot in the snow where she'd lost it earlier. There were fresh car tracks in the driveway of what he guessed was the ambulance, and police.

Dalton pulled up the drive and saw Meg standing there in the open door waiting for him. He climbed from the truck as she ran out to him, and they embraced.

"I can't do this!" Meg sobbed. "I can't do this Dalton, oh god!"

Dalton held her tight and walked her into the house.

Inside Hank lay next to Charlie's chair with his head down, watching Dalton and Meg—then looked to the door as if Charlie would be the next to come through.

Dalton sat next to Meg on the couch, and she held her hands over her eyes as if to hold back the tears, and she sobbed and moaned with grief. She loved Charlie more than she ever loved herself, and Dalton knew that part of Meg was dying as well.

They sat on the couch for hours, and eventually Dalton walked Meg back to her bedroom, and he had her lie down. She appeared to have calmed down, but the silent tears continued to stream down her face. Dalton put an afghan over her, and sat next to her on the edge of the bed. He put his hand on her forehead and gently pushed her hair back, and Meg smiled sheepishly.

"You remind me so much of Daddy," she said. Dalton returned the sheepish smile.

"I think you saw a side of him us boys never saw," Dalton said. "He was always to busy chasing us around with a switch." This made Meg laugh a little, and smile. She took a deep breath.

"I'm not ready for this," Meg said.

"I know," Dalton said, "Your going to be all right. Your tougher than the lot of us."

"I don't know about that," Meg said.

"I'll be here to help as much as I can," Dalton said.

"I'm supposed to be taking care of you!" Meg cried.

"Well, you'll have plenty of time for that," said Dalton.

"What will I do when you're gone?" Meg said through more tears.

"One day at a time," Dalton said.

He stayed there with her till she fell asleep, while Hank stayed out in the front room watching the door, waiting for Charlie.

Twenty-three

The next morning Dalton sat alone in the kitchen while Meg showered. The house seemed so empty without Charlie. Hank came into the kitchen and fell into a pile at Dalton's feet. Dalton could tell day by day that the pain was getting worse in his groin and lower back, it was harder to mask it with booze and painkillers.

Meg got out of the shower and dressed, and when she came into the kitchen they sat around the table in silence.

"Had you and Charlie ever talked about this?" Dalton asked.

"Yes, everything's already taken care of," Meg said. "About ten years ago Charlie planned everything out—cemetery plots, everything. It's even all paid for."

"Really?" Dalton was surprised.

"He never told you about all that?" Meg asked.

"He may have, I don't remember."

"We got the plots close to Mama and Daddy," Meg said. "Have you ever thought about any of this?"

"No," Dalton said. "Oh, I have a Will, but never gave any of the other much thought."

"Life sure has gone fast," Meg said.

"Not over quite yet," Dalton said.

"Feels like its coming to a close fast." Meg said.

Dalton didn't know what to say. He wanted to comfort Meg, but this morning his thoughts were consumed with his own death—his ending, and resolving this life. Time was running out, like an hourglass or setting sun.

Dalton stood up slowly, "I have to go feed Sam, and shower. I'll be back in a few hours."

"Can I go with you?" Meg asked.

"Well, sure," Dalton said. He hadn't thought off asking her to come over, but it was a good idea.

Dalton, Meg, and Hank got into the old truck and drove out to the house on Cathead Bay. Dalton was glad she was with him, and maybe it was good for her to spend a little time at the place where she was raised, surrounded by old familiar ghosts.

When they got there Hank was the first in, then Dalton, and Meg. Sam sat on the edge of the table.

"Morning Sam," Dalton said, and scratched him on top of the head as he passed. "Meg why don't you go sit down and rest for a while." But she looked a little uncomfortable being idle.

"Look at this kitchen Dalton," she said, "What would Mama say," as she went to straightening and drawing some hot dish water. Dalton looked around and didn't think it looked that bad, but he also knew his sister and that this was as close to relaxed she could get—and if she was just to sit she would only dwell on the reality of the moment.

He watched her as she nervously wiped off the counter and around the sink. He loved his sister dearly, she had been the only person in his life who remained consistently involved, and loved him unconditionally. In dealing with his own mortality—the thought of leaving his sister alone in this life is what bothered him the most.

"I'm going upstairs to bathe," Dalton said.

"Okay, I'll see if I can find something for lunch."

"Alright," Dalton said watching her move about the kitchen. "I love you Meg." She turned towards Dalton with tears in her eyes and a slight smile, and nodded her head—she couldn't speak, she was hurting so bad inside; then went back to wiping the counter-top. Dalton slowly went up the stairs.

In the bathroom at the top of the stairs he drew a hot bath, and undressed as Sam watched from the wooden stool. Dalton sat a whiskey bottle next to the tub, it was about half full—it was enough.

He tried to urinate, but it hurt—only a few drops came out. He stepped into the hot bath and it burned his feet. He lowered himself into the water and leaned back. He took a long drink from the bottle. Sam was cleaning himself, purring a little.

Dalton took another long drink, then set the bottle on the edge of the tub and closed his eyes. He thought about his last conversation with Charlie, and envisioned him walking away into the dark. Dalton wondered what Charlie's last thoughts were, and couldn't remember if he'd ever told Charlie that he loved him too.

Twenty-four

In New York, Dan and Julie were just walking up the steps of the Astor Place subway station when his cell phone rang. He looked at it, and saw it was his Dad—he almost didn't answer it—but was running low on cash, and needed to talk to him anyway. So he answered the cell.

"Hello?"

"Dan—It's Dad," Dalton said.

"Hi Dad."

"I have some bad news," Dalton said. "Your uncle Charlie passed away last night." Dan was quiet for a moment. He felt guilty because he knew this should mean more to him—it should make him feel terrible, but it didn't. He didn't really know Charlie well, besides from what his mother had told him—that Charlie was a drunk and never did anything with his life.

"Oh Dad, I'm sorry. How's aunt Meg?" Dan asked, for Dalton's sake.

"She's pretty tore up," Dalton said. "Can you come home for the funeral?"

Dan hesitated.

Dalton waited.

"Well, I can. I'm pretty short on cash—it might be tough."

Dalton starred out the window towards the bay, watching the waves. He heard what Dan said, and knew this was a pattern with his son that he'd created. Dalton's good fortune had enabled Dan to become this. It made Dalton sad, but he wanted him to come home.

"I'll take care of the plane ticket—don't worry about that—just come home."

"Okay Dad. I'll make the arrangements and call you later." Dalton nodded as if Dan could see him. He wanted to tell Dan that he loved him, but he didn't, he said goodbye, and hung up the phone.

Dan closed his cell phone as he and Julie walked down St. Marks place.

"My uncle died," Dan said to Julie, "Dad wants me to come home."

"What?" Julie said indignantly. "What about my parents?" She said.

"What about them?" Dan said.

"They'll be here in two days—they're coming to meet you!"

"My uncle died!" Dan said defensively. "Dad wants me to come home!"

"What uncle? Do you even know him?" Julie said.

"Fuck you!" he said, "If Dad wants me to come home—I'm going home!"

"Afraid he'll cut you out of the will," she said.

Dan stopped walking. She turned and looked at him. "My parents are flying all the way from Tampa to meet you—and this means so much to me—and now your going to take a trip home!"

"For a funeral!" Dan said. They were both getting loud and people were stepping around them on the street.

"I suppose you'll make time to see some old girlfriends while your home,' Julie said as she turned and walked away.

"Fuck you!" Dan said louder—but she kept walking away, back towards their apartment that Dalton was paying for.

Dan went to the Tavern and got drunk.

Twenty-five

The day of the funeral Dalton was up at 4:30 A.M. and took a hot bath. Sam sat on the bed watching while he put on his suit. Dalton straightened he and Lilly's wedding photo on the wall, then went downstairs. Meg was up and dressed, sitting in the living room looking out the picture window. Hank was at her feet. Dalton went and sat next to her.

"Remember Mama's funeral?" she said, "It was cold like this. Remember the old reverend cut the prayer at the grave short cause he was so cold."

"I remember," Dalton said. They were both quiet for a moment. Sam jumped up on the couch between them.

"Remember how Daddy disliked Charlie," she smiled through tears, "How tough he was on him at first. He'd always say 'you can do better,' and 'why would you marry that man!' But then, eventually, Charlie won him over."

"With booze I think," Dalton said. Meg laughed, wiping tears away.

"He did keep daddy drunk there for a while."

"Thank god Ma wasn't around then," Dalton said.

"She would have killed them both!" Meg laughed.

"Remember when dad wanted to take Charlie fishing?" Dalton said.

"And they both fell into the lake trying to get into the boat," Meg laughed harder, wiping away more tears.

"I think they were friends ever-after that." Dalton said. They both laughed and she wiped her eyes again. "He was a good man."

"And a good husband," Meg said.

"He sure loved you," said Dalton. He reached out and took hold of Meg's hand.

"I know he did," she said.

They sat there for several hours, when Dalton finally asked her if she was ready to go. They went out the back door through the snow to the old truck, Hank and Sam sat together watching out the big picture window as they dove away.

Twenty-six

The funeral home was the same one they used when their father passed away years ago. Fred Anderson, the man who ran the place was an old friend to the Jones family, and was standing at the door to greet them when they arrived. Dalton shook Fred's hand as they walked through the front door. Fred embraced Meg, and led her back to the room where Charlie was. Dalton followed.

They walked up to the casket and there was Charlie.

"I never saw him in that suit," Dalton said.

"It was his good suit," Meg said, half laughing, half crying, "He never wore it. He said he was afraid if he wore it out he'd just have to go buy another one to be buried in."

Dalton wanted to laugh—but couldn't.

"He looks peaceful," Meg said. Dalton stood there and held his sister's hand, and watched as she stared at her dead husband. Dalton was surprised how calm she'd become, and that she was holding herself together so well. Even as tears were streaming down her face she seemed stoic and strong. This was a side of her he'd never really seen before—perhaps because Charlie was always the strong one who dealt with the hard stuff, and she could be vulnerable.

Now she needed to be strong.

Twenty-seven

All kinds of people started to arrive. Some of them came up to Dalton and shook his hand, said they were sorry, and Dalton said thank you. He kept an eye on Meg who was surrounded by a crowd, hugging, kissing, and holding on to them. He thought how it seemed more like a Sunday social than his best friends funeral, people were laughing, patting each other on the back, a few tears. A group of men and women stood outside smoking cigarettes—Eugene Wixson was one of them, he was all dressed up in a black suit. There were some teenagers gathered out in the parking lot. Reverend James Howard from the Methodist church arrived and smelled like booze—he, Eugene, and Charlie fished and drank together. James had tears in his eyes as he went to Meg—then to Charlie.

Eugene finished smoking and stepped inside. He smelled like booze too. Dalton shook his hand, and thought about how Eugene had buried half his clientele over the last forty-years.

More people arrived and the old funeral home was filling up. Dalton wondered if he'd get quite as big a turn out when his day came.

While looking the crowd over for Meg, someone squeezed his elbow, he turned and it was Dan, and Lilly. Dalton was shocked. Speechless. Dan gave him a hug, then Lilly. When she hugged him Dalton hung on for a few extra seconds.

"You okay?" Lilly asked.

"I didn't know you were coming," Dalton said.

"How's Meg?" she said.

"Being brave today—tomorrow will be tough." Lilly took Dalton's hand and squeezed it hard while looking him over.

"Are you okay?" She asked again. "You don't look well." Dalton almost told her about the cancer right then, but hesitated and decided that this was absolutely the worst time.

"I'm all right," he said, but Lilly knew he wasn't.

The service was long, and Reverend Howard talked about Charlie, God, and Heaven. He read from the Bible, and a man from the Methodist church got up with a guitar and sang the old gospel song *Where We Never Grow Old*.

Meg asked Dan to be one of the pallbearers, he was surprised, and said yes. They carried the coffin to the hearse, and all drove in a long procession to the cemetery. It was cold, and gray clouds filled the sky—it was going to snow. The wind seemed to die down as everyone followed the pallbearers carrying the casket to the grave. Everything was surreal. Reverend Howard said a few more words and invited everyone back to the church for lunch and coffee. Dalton stood next to Meg, and she hugged everyone before they walked away. Dan and Lilly stood close behind them.

From the crowd emerged Angie and Billy—she went up to Dalton and hugged him. "I'm sorry Dalton," she said. Billy reached out and tugged at Dalton's coat sleeve.

"I'm sorry Mr. Jones," he said.

"Thank you Billy," Dalton said, then he looked to Angie. "Thank you." Dalton turned to Meg, "Meg—you remember Angie Bartlett and Billy." Meg hugged them both, and when Angie turned from Meg she saw Dan for the first time that day, and felt weak—like she was going to get sick. She didn't know if she wanted to embrace him, or to run as fast as she could away from him. They both stood there frozen without words. Billy took a hold of Angie's hand, and she looked down—then back to Dan. Lilly stepped forward…

"Hello Angela," Lilly said. "Who might this be?" Referring to Billy. Angie knew Lilly didn't like her, never did. Angie always felt like she and Lilly competed for Dan's attention and love.

"This is my son," Angie said, looking back to Dan.

"I didn't know you had a baby, where's your husband? I'd love to meet him." Lilly said.

"I'm not married. It's just me and Billy."

"Oh," Lilly said, judging Angie, "I see." Angie turned to Dan.

"Hi Dan."

"Hi," he said feeling his face go flush. Billy tugged on Angie's arm.

"Mom, who are they?"

"This is… an old friend of mine, he's Mr. Jones' son—and this is his mother." Billy looked perplexed for a moment, and looked up to Lilly.

"Were you married to Mr. Jones?" Billy asked.

"Yes, I was a long time ago."

"Are you the one who took all his furniture?"

Everyone froze.

Dalton wanted to laugh.

Angie was horrified.

"Oh Billy!" She said, "We better go—good to see you both," and she pulled Billy away quickly into the crowd. Lilly didn't know what to say, and Dan was still in shock from seeing Angie, and her son.

This was the first time he'd seen her since he'd left Northport—and the first time he'd ever known Billy existed.

Lilly watched them as they walked away and said, "Doesn't seem like she's done too much with her life, it's a shame." Dan just looked at Lilly with a blank stare. At times he felt like he didn't know his mother at all, this was one of those times.

Dalton walked Meg back towards the old truck and helped her inside the cab. He turned on the heater and it blew warm air on their feet and legs. Meg wiped her eyes and was quiet. They drove slowly through the cemetery and it started to snow, blowing and swirling around. They didn't talk the entire way to the church, and when they arrived she took a deep breath and let out a long sigh.

"You ready?" Dalton asked.

"I guess so," Meg said. "I'm ready to go home."

"You want to go?" Dalton said, ready to put the truck back in gear.

"No, were almost done," Meg said.

"You want to stay out at the house again tonight?"

"No, I think I want to go home."

"Do you want me to stay over?"

"No. I'm so tired, and I think I want to be alone tonight."

"You sure?"

"Yes, I'm sure," Meg said.

"Alright."

Before they got out of the truck Meg took another deep breath, and as they walked into the church Dalton hung on to her tight.

The afternoon went fast, lots of casual conversation, handshakes, hugs. Lots more people came up and introduced themselves, said that they were sorry, and going to miss Charlie.

Dalton was surprised at how many people Charlie knew—but Charlie was that kind of guy, you'd meet him once and you would walk away feeling like you had been friends with him for years.

As everyone was preparing to leave, Meg thanked Reverend Howard, and the ladies who prepared lunch. Dalton went over to Dan and Lilly who were sitting at the table near the door.

"Where are you staying tonight?" he asked.

"No plans yet, but I think we'll head back to Traverse City," Lilly said.

"Why not stay at the house?" Dalton said. Lilly hesitated, and seemed a little uncomfortable with the thought. "It's not like I'm asking you to move back in."

"Alright," she said hesitantly.

"Sounds good to me," Dan said.

"Make yourselves at home," Dalton said. "We're going to get Hank, Meg's dog, and then I'm going to take her home. I'll see you later."

"Alright," Dan said.

"If there's anything special you want, you better pick it up—there's not much out there."

Twenty-eight

That evening Dan helped Dalton light a fire in the fireplace and Lilly went upstairs to make up the spare bed. "Dalton," she yelled down stairs, "do you have any more clean sheets?"

"In the bedroom closet—where you left them," he said. Lilly paused, and then went to the bedroom. She got the sheets out of the closet, and as she walked out of the room she noticed she and Dalton's wedding photo still hanging above his dresser. She was standing there staring at it when Dalton stepped into the room.

"Find them?" he asked.

"Yeah," she said. "I'm surprised you still have that up."

"Why would I take it down?" he said, then reached up and straightened the photo on the wall, and went back downstairs leaving Lilly standing there with the folded sheets in their old bedroom.

Twilight passed and outside the snow continued to fall. Lilly called Walter who was back home in New York. Once she was off the phone they all gathered around the fireplace in the living room—the lights were dim and they watched the hot embers of the fire snap and pop. They all had several drinks, and Lilly would have the occasional cigarette. Across the room from her Sam sat next to Dalton glaring at Lilly.

"I can't believe that cat won't even let me pet him," Lilly said.

"There not as forgiving as people," Dalton said.

Lilly ignored him and lit another cigarette. She was the only woman Dalton knew who could still make smoking look sexy. Dalton leaned back and shut his eyes. He knew this would be the perfect time to tell them about the cancer. In a few moments, perhaps he would, he just wanted to sit here a little longer.

"I was surprised to see Angie today," Lilly said. "I'm not sure why she came." She turned to Dan, "I'm so glad you two didn't stay together—if you would have you'd probably be stuck here with her." Dan said nothing, just watched the fire, and Dalton was somewhere else all together.

"Dalton?" Lilly said for the second time.

"Yes?" He opened his eyes.

"Why would Angela come to the funeral today?"

"Because we're friends, Lilly."

"You and her?"

"Yes Lilly—Angie and I are friends."

"Your not…" she started to insinuate more than friends.

"Oh *Jesus Christ*, no! I'm twice her age for *god* sake!"

"Well, you're all alone, and have a lot of money, everyone knows that."

"God damnit Lilly, she's not after my money—besides trying to help her with anything is like pulling teeth."

"Why are you helping her Dad?" Dan asked. Dalton was starting to feel cornered, and between the pain in his back, strained emotions of the day, the pain killers, and the whiskey—he snapped…

"What the hell is it to you—you'll still get your inheritance!"

"What does that mean?" Dan said.

"*Jesus*, Dan—your a grown man and still sucking from the hind-tit!"

"Now boys!" Lilly tried to interrupt.

"Your living beyond your means!" Dalton continued, "I pay for that apartment! I still give you an allowance for god sake! When I was your age I was on my own, and if anything I was helping my old man out!"

"Your father couldn't afford to help you Dalton," Lilly said. Sam jumped down from next to Dalton and ran up stairs. "Would you rather see Dan living here with that… that girl, and kids, and have to fight for everything like you did?"

"That girl's name is Angie—and that kid of hers is *probably your grandson*! And everything I worked for built character. And strength! What the hell does Dan have to show for living off me all these years?"

"What do you mean *grandson*?" Lilly said. Then she looked to Dan.

"Oh hell," Dalton said, "the entire town thinks he's Dan's son, they've been whispering about it for years! He was born right after Dan took off for New York," Dalton said.

"If you knew this why the hell didn't you say something?" Dan said.

"Would you have come home? Hell, the only time I ever talked to you the first years you were gone was when you needed money!"

"But you could've said something!" Dan said.

"It wasn't my place,' Dalton said.

"What the hell do you mean is wasn't your place?" Lilly said as she stood up, then Dan stood up.

"If Angie wanted you to know, she would've told you herself!" Dalton said. "I've tried to talk to you about her and you always shut me down!"

"I was trying to get on with my life!" Dan said.

"You were running away!" Dalton yelled.

"What was he running from Dalton?" Lilly yelled, "What?"

"From life—responsibility—his family!" Dalton said.

"What family Dalton?" Lilly said, "I was in New York, and his father was a reclusive drunk!"

Dalton stood up, but the pain in his lower back and groin was so intense he had to lean against the chair he'd been sitting in. Dan was pacing back and forth, and Lilly franticly lit another cigarette.

"I should've known better than to think that we could spend a quiet evening together," Lilly said.

Dan spun around and threw his glass at the wall, it shattered— glass, ice, and whiskey went everywhere.

"You people are killing me! I've tried! I've tried! Do you know what its like being *Dalton Jones' son*? The expectations—and the disappointment when people find out I'm not you! Do you know what it's been like all my life listening to you two fight? Listening to you bad mouth my father? And you locking yourself away—you never even tried when I was a kid, Dad! Where were you? Then you, Mom—running away to New York the way you did, leaving me here with him—it wasn't easy!"

"It wasn't easy on me either Dan!" Lilly shouted.

"But you were a grown woman—and I was just a kid—and you left!"

"Because your father had been fucking around! Wouldn't you leave? Wouldn't you do the same thing?"

"God dammit—how many times do I have to hear this? Regardless he's still my father—it hurts me when you tear him down!" Dan said to Lilly. Then he turned back to Dalton, "And you say nothing—you just gave me money when all I ever wanted was a Dad!" Dan said, then he turned, rushed out of the house, and slammed the door.

Though the front window Lilly and Dalton watched the taillights of the rental car disappear down the long driveway. Dalton looked at Lilly who was taking the last long drag off her cigarette. He looked at the broken glass and mess, and started walking upstairs.

"God damn you Dalton,' she said, "Where are you going?"

"Upstairs."

"Look what you've done—why didn't you tell us about that boy? Why do you have to be such a miserable son-of-a-bitch! You've ruined my life—our son's life—and do you even care? Do you have any remorse? I wish you could show a little emotion for once in your life you old *son-of-a-bitch*!"

Dalton barely made it up the stairs. He hung onto the handrail and broke out into a cold sweat. Once in the bathroom he sat down on the toilet with a closed lid and rested. It had been a terrible day, one of the worst.

He drew a hot bath and noticed a cats paw under the door—he opened the door a crack and Sam hurried in, rubbed against Dalton's leg and hopped up on the wooden stool by the tub.

Dalton undressed, and took a couple of the painkillers the doctor gave him, then sunk into the hot bath. It took him a long time just to sit down in the tub he hurt so bad. He sat still for a while—just breathing. He drank a little whiskey, and waited for the pain pills to start working.

He should've told Lilly and Dan about the cancer, but in a way he was glad they all aired their emotions and frustrations. Everyone had been holding back for too long, and better to come out now cause when he's dead and gone it would just fester inside them.

What a terrible day he thought. Dalton was glad Meg decided not to come over, and wondered how she was doing.

He realized he'd let it all get to him today—an accumulation of everything: the cancer; loosing his best friend; and being sur-rounded by these emotionally charged people. As he relaxed he was able to urinate in the warm bath water without it hurting as much, it was a relief, and he sighed. Sam hopped down off the stool and curled up on the bathroom rug—Dalton could hear him purring.

Twenty-nine

It was dark as Dan drove the icy winding roads into Northport. He stopped at a party store and bought a pint of whiskey. Before he started the car back up he downed about a third of the pint. He was so angry, and hated that his parents were able to get him to lose control like that, like a kid throwing a tantrum.

The more he dwelled on it the madder he got and the faster he drove, winding around the corner and down the hill into town. He took the last curve to fast and slid off the road into a frozen snow bank.

Dan punched the dashboard of the car and cussed, he put the car in reverse, but he was just spinning the wheels. He got out and looked the car over, it wasn't going to move. He climbed back down into the drivers seat and drank more whiskey.

Once he calmed down a little he got out, slammed the door, and started walking into town. He passed Tom's Food Market, the Grandview, and up the hill towards the little house he and Angie used to share, so long ago. He wondered if she still lived there. His cell phone rang, it was his mother—he shut it off. He didn't want to talk to her, or his father.

He wondered how life got so screwed up, and if it would all be better if he distanced himself from both his parents, maybe move away or change his name.

Dan finished the pint of whiskey and dropped the empty bottle in the snow. Walking with his collar up and hands sunk deep into his pockets he finally got to the street where he used to live.

He stood there out in front of the house and could see Angie inside, and her son. Dan was surprised that she still lived there. It was a nice place for the price, and there wasn't a lot to choose from in Northport. He took a deep breath and went up to the door, and knocked. Angie pushed back the curtain, and was surprised to see Dan. She just stared at him for a moment, and he smiled. He desperately wanted to be invited in—to hide, and cry, and turn back time. When she opened the door Billy stood behind her.

"Hi," Dan said.

"Hi," said Angie.

"I was just in the neighborhood," he said. She didn't know what to say. Her heart was pounding. She had imagined this moment since the day Dan left—the day he'd come home.

"Are you drunk?" She asked. She knew he was without asking. In her imagination he didn't return like this.

"No—I had a drink—but—no, I'm not." He lied.

"What do you want Dan?"

"I just want to talk," he said looking sincerely pitiful. "We haven't talked in a long time." She looked at Billy behind her, and then back at Dan, then she opened the door and Dan stepped inside

"Did you walk here?" She asked as she shut the door.

"Part way," he said. He turned to Billy, "Hello again. I'm Dan. I'm not sure if you remember me?"

"I remember you," Billy said. "Your Mr. Jones's son."

Dan laughed, "Yeah, that's me."

"Billy, why don't you go play in your room for a while and let Dan and I talk." Billy hesitated, but said okay, and went into his little bedroom.

"Want some coffee?" Angie asked Dan.

"No, I'm fine."

"It's been a long time Dan."

"I know," he said looking at the floor.

"What's going on?"

"Well, it's been a really awful day."

"We all have bad days, Dan."

"I just wanted to talk—after I saw you today—I just felt…" he wasn't sure how to finish the sentence. He thought she was as beautiful as ever. He wanted to hold her, to kiss her on the mouth. What he didn't know was that she was feeling the exact same way—but for her it was mixed with guilt and regret. Seeing him reminded her of her own mistakes and weakness. Ignorance and youth go hand in hand she thought. She'd never change the past, because she loves her son too much, but she'd always known that she was once on a different path that she abandoned by her choices.

Angie wanted nothing more than to take Dan in her arms, and hold him, make love with him and go back in time—erase the bad times, and all the time apart. He was her first love, and she still loved him.

"Can I take your coat?" Angie asked. "Why don't you sit down."

Dan sat down on the sofa.

"You want a beer or something?"

"Sure," he said. He watched her walk across the room and dig a couple cold cans of beer out of the back of the fridge. She came back and sat down next to him.

"Thanks," he said, and took a sip.

"So, pretty terrible day?"

"Yeah," Dan said. "In a lot of ways. I always try to see the good that might come out of bad situations, but it hasn't worked today."

"How's your Dad?"

"He's pretty tore up."

"How was it being back in Northport, with he and your mother?"

"Terrible," Dan said. He went on to elaborate some, and it lead to a two-hour conversation.

At 10:30 P.M. Angie tucked Billy into bed, but before he laid down Billy came out and said good night to Dan. Angie stayed in the bedroom for a while talking to Billy, and when she came out she shut his bedroom door softly.

"You want another beer?" she asked. Dan said he would if she would. They continued their conversation for another hour, and in the back of both of their minds they wanted this night to end the same.

They laughed and talked about family, and some of their old friends. Dan watched her smile and laugh, and brush her hair from her eyes. Around midnight he leaned forward and kissed her. At first she was still, but then she kissed him back. He leaned over her and kissed her on the neck and face. She led him into her bedroom and they made love on the floor next to the bed, and afterwards she cried, but it was dark and Dan never knew.

Thirty

Dalton walked back downstairs and found Lilly sitting at the kitchen table next to his closed journal. She took a long drag off her cigarette when he walked into the room. He noticed that she didn't look as attractive smoking now—she looked old, nervous and addicted.

"Do you know, over the years, how often I've wanted to read what you wrote in there?"

"Did you ever?"

"No," she said. "I should have." Dalton sat down across from her at the table. Sam had followed him down, but when he saw Lilly he went back upstairs.

"Dan call?" Dalton asked.

"No," she said. "He won't." The kitchen smelled like smoke from her cigarettes, and from the fireplace. As they sat there the refrigerator's motor started to hum. The clock on the wall ticked.

"I'm sorry about tonight," Dalton said. Lilly was shocked, an apology was so unlike Dalton.

"What, are you dying?" Lilly said in jest—Dalton looked startled.

"What?" he said.

"An apology—your getting soft in your old age Mr. Jones," she said and lit another cigarette.

Dalton knew there would never be a better time. The words welled up in his throat. His mouth was dry, and his heart began to beat faster.

"Lilly," he said, "I have cancer. Prostate cancer. I've decided not to go through the treatment—to let it run its course." Lilly was stunned and just sat there for a long time holding her smoldering cigarette.

"Run its course?" she finally said.

"Yeah," said Dalton. She just stared at him. "I've been through all the tests and the cancer has metastasized and spread. Even if I went through the treatments it would only prolong the inevitable."

"So you're going to do nothing?"

"Lilly, it's too late. It wouldn't matter. I've chosen this… or how to deal with this at least." She sat there in the dark and took another long drag off her cigarette.

"It's just like you to do nothing as everything around you falls apart. What about your family—can't you even try for them?"

"What family?" he said defensively. "If I wasn't handing Dan money every month, I don't even know if he would talk to me. My wife lives in New York and spends her nights with another man. My best friend is dead. The only ones I am concerned about is Meg, and that god damn cat."

Dalton paused and pressed on his temple in frustration.

"I'm gonna die Lilly."

Lilly thought about all the wasted time, the hurtful words, and the divorce. Hesitantly she reached across the table and took his hand. For the first time in years they both felt safe with the other, safe to be nothing but what they were, and inwardly regretting all the mistakes that tore them apart.

Thirty-one

Angie woke up to Dan caressing her naked body. She smiled and moved up against him. "This feels like a dream," she said. He smiled.

"It's been so long, I'd almost forgotten how safe I feel with you—how perfect you are." Dan said as he continued to caress her face, breasts, and hip—she hadn't changed in all these years.

"Can I ask you something?" Dan asked as he brushed the hair from her eyes.

"Of course," she said. He appeared nervous, and she wondered if this was it—what she dreamed of so often? Was he going to ask to come home? Did he still love her and want to be together again? Her stomach turned in circles, hesitant, anxiously awaiting his question.

Dan was feeling the same way, and after a moment he just blurted it out.

"Is Billy… am I Billy's father?" And as he asked the question he realized he desperately wanted to be the boys father, and how much he still loved Angie. He could easily fall back into a life with her here, anywhere. Dan's past, present, and future all seemed to swell up into that moment, and hung onto what ever her response might be.

Angie began to cry, it wasn't what she had hoped for. It was the one question she hoped he wouldn't ask. She didn't want to drudge up the past tonight, only look forward. But here it was.

"You're not Dan," she whispered. Dan instantly went cold and recoiled. "I'm so sorry—I'm so sorry," she said, and the past was alive again, and all the guilt and regret resurfaced. Dan lay there on his back for a moment and said nothing.

"Dan, talk to me, please, what are you feeling?"

"I wish you'd have said I was. I wish it was me."

Dan stood up in the dark room and gathered his clothes.

"Please don't go," Angie cried. "Please Dan."

Thirty-two

The telephone rang. Dalton and Lilly were back in the living room sitting in front of the fireplace. Dalton stood up from his chair and made his way to the kitchen to the phone.

"Hello?"

"Is it Dan?" Lilly asked.

"Dalton," it was Angie. "I'm so sorry for calling so late, but… Dan was here, when he left he was pretty upset. He didn't have a car and I'm not sure where he was going."

"What's going on?" Dalton said, confused. "What was he doing there this time of the night?" She didn't respond, but Dalton knew, and got mad. "You sound upset—were you fighting?"

"Oh Dalton, it doesn't matter—it was just the past all over again. Dan's upset and walked off, I can't go after him because of Billy, can you please?"

Dalton scowled, frustrated with Dan, angry with himself for loosing control this evening, for asking Lilly and Dan to come back here to the house, for not being with Meg, and for talking about Billy. Dalton hung up the phone. When he went to put on his boots Lilly jumped up from the couch.

"Where are you going? She asked, "What's happening?"

"I'm going to get Dan," Dalton said, and put on his coat. Lilly grabbed her coat and followed him out the back door.

"Stay here," Dalton said.

Lilly lit another cigarette as she watched Dalton get into the truck. She blew smoke in the direction of the taillights as he pulled out of the long driveway.

Thirty-three

Dalton stopped in the middle of the road when he saw Dan's rental car in the snow bank with flashers blinking. Dalton flashed the trucks hi-beams, but didn't see Dan. He drove into town past Angie's place, her light was still on, but Dalton didn't stop. Then he drove back towards Main Street, there was only one other place he could imagine Dan might be.

He parked across the street from the Grandview and walked through the slushy snow inside. It was quiet, and Eugene's grand-daughter Adley was behind the bar.

When she saw Dalton she pointed over to a figure at the end of the bar—it was Dan slumped over his drink. Dalton was angry, and strode over to Dan, reached out and grabbed his shoulder, and jerked him off the bar stool onto the floor.

"You miserable little son-of-a-bitch!" Dalton yelled. "You had to go over there didn't you!" Dan started to get back on his feet. "Haven't you done enough to that poor girl, running out on her the way you did, and now this! Couldn't you just leave it be!" Dan stood up in front of Dalton equally as mad. Dalton clinched his fists.

"How could I after what you said!" Dan yelled back. "And for your information—he's *not* my son—*not* your grandson, Dad—so you can stop pretending to be the fucking hero—swooping in and picking up all the pieces your dead beat son left behind! Did she ever tell you why I ran off and left her? Have you ever asked me why I left when I did? I caught her fucking my best friend—I caught them in my bed! He's Billy's father—not me!"

"I didn't know," Dalton said.

"Don't you think I wish he was mine? I lost dad—and when I lost her, I had nothing else left here—god knows you weren't available!"

"You can't run from it all your life," Dalton said sternly.

"Listen to you—you old bastard!"

No one spoke to Dalton that way—no one—and with a weighty clinched fist he punched Dan in the mouth knocking him back against the bar, to the floor. Several guys jumped up, but didn't touch Dalton who was standing over Dan like a raging bull.

Dalton turned and walked out of the bar.

After Dalton left the Grandview Dan picked himself up off the floor. He wanted to run out of there, but realized he had no place to go. He picked up the stool he'd fallen from and sat back down at the bar.

Adley poured another drink and set it in front of him.

"On the house," she said, and poured herself a shot.

"Thanks."

"Cheers," she said, and Dan lifted his glass. "That was the most excitement I've ever seen in here, people will be talking about that for a long time," Adley said.

"Great," Dan said.

"Never seen your old man like that before."

"Me neither," Dan said rubbing his lip and jaw.

"My name's Adley," she said, and stuck her hand out to shake his hand. "I'm Eugene's granddaughter."

"Nice to meet you," Dan said. "I'm Dan, Dan Jones."

"You want some ice for that lip?" she asked.

"No," Dan said, "I'll be fine."

Before too long the regular late night murmur returned, people came and went, and someone started playing Christmas music on the Jukebox.

Dan sat there till closing time. He drank and talked to Adley between her pouring beers and brief conversation with the last few locals still hanging on to the bar. When the last two shuffled out, she started to shut off the lights. Dan stood up and put on his coat.

"Are you all right to drive?" Adley asked.

"No, I don't think so," Dan said. "Doesn't matter much anyhow, I put my car in the ditch a few hours ago."

"So you couldn't drive even if you wanted too."

"Right." Adley shut off the last of the lights, and followed Dan towards the door. Dan stepped outside as she locked the front door.

"Would you like a ride home… or anywhere?"

"Anywheres a better place to be."

Thirty-four

Dalton slept till 7:45 A.M., then laid in bed with old Sam—who was sprawled out next to him for another hour. When he heard a car pull in the driveway Dalton climbed out of the bed and looked out the window. He recognized Eugene's granddaughter, Adley, and watched what looked like an awkward goodbye between her and Dan as he climbed out of her car. Dalton looked down at his bruised hand and knuckles, and wished last night had all been a bad dream.

Outside, Dan was still getting out of Adley's car, "Thanks again for letting me crash at your place last night, I appreciate it."

"No problem. Your Dads our best customer, it was the least I could do," Adley said, and smiled. "I would've loved to have seen my Grandpa Eugene's face when he found you on the couch this morning."

"Yeah… I think I surprised him," Dan said. "Well, it was good to meet you—I wish it would've been under different circumstances."

"Well, life rarely works out as well as we imagine it should," Adley said.

"Isn't that the truth," Dan said. "Thanks Adley. We've had the most honest conversation that I've had in years—with anyone," Dan said.

"That's sad. You did all the talking. Maybe you're finally just being honest with yourself," Adley said. "Come back again sometime Mr. Jones and I'll buy you another drink."

"I'll take you up on that," Dan said. "See you around." They shook hands, he climbed out of the car, and watched her drive away.

By the time Dalton got dressed and went down stairs, Dan was back outside paying the tow truck driver who had arrived with the rental car in tow.

As the tow-truck pulled out of the drive-way Dan came inside and took off his shoes. Dalton stepped into the kitchen and they stared at one another in silence.

"I'm leaving today," Dan said. Dalton stepped toward Dan and handed him a check. Dan looked at it, and had to do a double take because it was for such a large amount. "What is this?"

"Your inheritance," Dalton said.

"What?"

"It's time for you to find your own way. I don't want you to feel obligated to talk to me anymore. It's your money—you'll get it sooner or later. Now you're free to go live your life, no strings attached."

Dan was mad at first, then overwhelmed with sadness.

"So that's it?" Dan said, "We're all done?"

"Yep," Dalton said putting his hands in his pockets. "All done. Sorry I was such a lousy father," Dalton said. He walked past Dan, out the door to his truck, and drove away.

Dalton didn't know where he was going when he left the house, but in a few minutes he pulled into Meg's driveway. She opened the front door as he walked up the steps, Hank barked and wagged his tail. When Dalton hugged Meg the tears welled up in her eyes, and she wiped them away with her apron.

"You want some coffee?" she asked. He said he did and followed her to the kitchen.

"How are you doing?" Dalton asked, she wiped another stray tear from her cheek.

"I'm gonna be okay," she said. "I just can't stop going, you know… I'm scared. I'm sad. I feel like there was so much more Charlie and I needed to share, so many more things we never got to do that we always talked about.

We were going to go back up to Mackinaw in the spring and stay in that bed and breakfast that we liked so much. He always wanted to go to California and see the Redwoods, and to Texas to see the Alamo. We were going to paint the living room and buy new curtains." She poured them both coffee, and sat down at the kitchen table, and wiped her face with her apron again.

"You can still get new curtains," Dalton said.

"Oh, I know—it just doesn't seem as important now."

They sat there and drank coffee in silence. The sunlight lit up the room, and Dalton could smell the vanilla scented lotion that Meg used.

Meg was a lot stronger than he ever gave her credit for, and it would be her who he'd soon be leaning on. In many ways he already was, running to her, escaping his own home and life. They needed one another.

"Life hasn't been fair to me," Meg said holding her coffee mug, staring out the window. This surprised Dalton coming from Meg—it was rare she ever said anything negative or unpleasant. "When I was younger, all I ever wanted was a family, a big family, and children. You know, Charlie and I tried when we were first married—but I was too old, and it just never took. I had those miscarriages, you know, and after you go through that a few times you just kind of lose hope. Then when we came to terms with that, Charlie and I had some problems."

"I didn't know," Dalton said.

"We didn't talk about it. He left once for about a week, it was terrible, and I cried."

"Where was I?" said Dalton.

"It was back when you were still in New York, before you moved back. Those were tough times, but you know, after that week away he came home, and was nothing but wonderful the rest of the time we were together."

She wiped her face with her apron again.

"But I always dreamt of that big happy family. When you came back and brought Lilly and Dan, I imagined these big family dinners on Sundays, and I, well… then soon after you and Lilly started having trouble, and you were drinking…

Charlie was a good husband. He was always good to me, and I know he loved me, but a lot of the time it seemed he rather be sitting up at the Grandview talking to strangers than to be here with me.

I've spent a lot of time alone. It seems like the more I wished for things the further they got away from me.

But, you know, once you came around, you have been my saving grace. You've given me a bit of what I always longed for—by letting me in—by coming around, stopping over and having coffee with me. When you were around, Charlie would get out of his chair and sit here and talk, and for moments, everything seemed to be like what I always wanted—oh, we didn't have all the kids—but you were here, and I've always loved you so much." Meg said and wiped her face again.

"I was eleven when you were born, and thought Mama had you just for me. I used to carry you around on my hip, so proud and happy." She reached across the table and took Dalton's hand. "I guess I still am, and want you to know that I'm still here for you, and love you."

"Well, I know that Meg."

"You've always tried to protect me," she said, "but I'm tougher than you know. I know things are gonna get rough for you, and I want you to know that I'm here for you. No pride, no macho, and no modesty—I love you more than anything in the world, and I'm here to help, so let me. When you're ready—you just say so, and I'll be right there."

"God damn it Meg, I'm suppose to be the one here for you," Dalton said, and Meg laughed out loud through her tears. She got up and hugged her brother, and Hank barked and wagged his tail.

Thirty-five

Back at Dalton's house on Cathead Bay, Dan loaded he and Lilly's luggage into the rental car. Lilly watched him from Dalton's upstairs bedroom window. Lilly washed their sheets and towels and put them back in the bedroom closet. She looked at their old bed remembering so many nights of going to sleep alone, those were sad and lonely times.

On her way out of the room she stopped and straightened her and Dalton's wedding photo that was still hanging on the wall. That was a lifetime ago she thought. She and Dalton were both so in love, he was so handsome and charming. A young talented author who literally had the world at his fingertips, and over time she watched it all slip away from him. The more he drank the less he wrote, and the worse it got, his moods, distance, and anger. He was a terrible father.

It was amazing that he was here in the house all those years, yet she felt like a single parent. Poor Dan suffered more so than Lilly. She was able to move on, but Dan would never have a chance for another Dad. Lilly loved Dalton, and hated him at the same time.

When she walked downstairs old Sam was sitting in Dalton's chair, but when he saw Lilly he jumped down and ran back upstairs.

"That god damn cat," she said to herself, and went on into the kitchen as Dan was coming back inside.

"I guess that's it," he said.

"Did you have a chance to talk to your Dad at all about what's going on?" she asked.

"What's going on?" Dan said.

"He has cancer Dan," Lilly said. "He's chosen not to have treatment. He told me last night after you left."

"He hasn't said anything," Dan said.

"Do you want to find him and talk to him before we leave?" Dan thought about it for a moment, first thinking yes, but then thought about last night and this morning.

"No," he said. "We should go."

"Are you sure? We can cancel the flight," Lilly said.

"I'm all set if you are," Dan said coldly. Lilly hated this, and Dalton for being a selfish son-of-a-bitch.

Lilly gathered her last few things, put on her coat, and started out to the car. Dan stepped back over to the table and laid the check down that Dalton had given him, shut off the light, and left.

Before he climbed into the rental car he looked back at the house for one final time. Dan had no intentions of ever returning.

Thirty-six

That afternoon Dalton fell asleep in Charlie's old recliner. Meg had pulled all the blinds and was sitting in her chair, legs covered by an afghan, and looking through old photo albums. Dalton woke himself up snoring, and as he opened his eyes he could feel the pain in his groin, lower back and legs; It was getting so bad.

He glanced over to Meg as she turned the pages of the old albums.

"What are you doing?" he asked.

"Remembering," she said.

"Where are you?"

"Home," Meg said. "Remember when we used to go ice fishing with Daddy, and how cold it was out there on the lake."

"He always had some brandy tucked away to sip on, to keep him warm," Dalton said.

"And you and Edward would fight as to who got to sit next to him, remember that?"

"I forgot about that," Dalton said. "If I recall you hated going ice fishing," Dalton said, and Meg laughed.

"I sure did, it was so cold. I'd always rather be in the house with Mama, cooking, sewing, or listening to the radio."

"I'd love to go back and be in that ice shanty with Daddy and Edward one more time," Dalton said.

"Wouldn't it be nice," Meg said.

"Sure would. Life got so complicated as we got older," Dalton said.

"Why is that?" said Meg.

"I don't really know. Age, spouses," Dalton said.

"Do you think about Edward much?" Meg asked.

"Yes," Dalton said, "All the time."

"I wish he could've grown old with us. Do you think he would've stayed around here?"

"Who knows," Dalton said.

Meg turned the page of the album to a portrait of Edward and Elizabeth.

"Elizabeth just drifted away, I never thought that would happen," said Meg.

"It was how she wanted it." Dalton said.

"It must have been horrible for her after Edward died," Meg said.

"I'm sure," said Dalton.

"She never liked Daddy too much. I always thought that she liked me, but who knows. Why do you think you and Edward always had so much trouble between the two of you?" Meg asked.

"Oh Meg, I don't know, stupid pride, ego. I always felt like he was jealous of me, like he didn't really care for me all that much. And he was so critical of everything I did."

"It was your drinking he didn't approve of," Meg said.

"It seemed like a lot more. I felt like we were eternally little kids fighting over stuff that just didn't matter. I felt like he put me down every chance he got. For a long time I tolerated it, but after a while I got tired of it."

"Do you ever think you made yourself feel that way because you were jealous of him, and all the attention Daddy and Mama gave him when he moved in. They were always praising him, trying to over compensate, I know you were jealous when you were a little boy.

When he went away to the war, people would come over and that was all they talked about—they'd say 'How's Edward, we sure miss him,' and I'd watch your expression change, and you know, you were drinking a lot back then too, and that changes things—how you remember—no matter what you say, it does.

Edward was hard on himself too, you know, he only held you up to those same standards. He saw what you were doing to yourself, and it hurt him. He wanted to say so much more to you, but he was a lot like Daddy in a lot of ways—a Jones through and through. He just didn't know how to express himself. He loved you dearly, but you know that," Meg said. "You were the closest one to him, you know." She looked over to Dalton whose head was hanging low as if all the weight of the world was on his shoulders. He knew Meg was right, and as the years passed he'd never stopped hurting over all the things he'd done. Dalton couldn't help but feel that if he'd of stayed away from Elizabeth, Edward would still be alive, that Edward's death was his fault. There would never be any resolution —that pain would never go away.

"I wish Edward would've lived longer," Meg said. "Men soften as they grow older, all those hard edges are worn down. If Edward would've lived, you two would've resolved all that tension a long time ago."

Dalton wished he'd have had that opportunity.

"Life hasn't been all that fair," Meg said. Dalton said nothing, just closed his eyes and leaned his head back, wishing he could go back and change everything, a lifetime of regret, and pain.

He'd been so selfish, and knew that he alone had caused so much damage, then, and now. His entire life he'd done nothing to stop his family from falling apart. If anything he'd been the main one who not only poured gasoline on the fires, but fanned the flames as well. Dalton thought if Meg only knew of the affair between he and Elizabeth, she'd never forgive him. As much as the cancer; the accumulation of so much pain and regret had been killing Dalton for years.

Thirty-seven

Dalton stayed with Meg all day then went home that night. He held his breath waiting to see if Lilly and Dan were still there, and was relieved that the house was dark and empty.

He went in through the back door, stomped his snow covered feet and turned on the lights. Old Sam sat there on the corner of the kitchen table, and Dalton scratched him on the head. The answering machine was blinking, and as he walked around the table to listen to it he noticed the check he'd wrote for Dan on the table. Dalton regretted doing that—he surely wasn't at his best.

He pushed the button on the answering machine, the first message was from Lilly...

"Dalton—I told Dan. I wish you would've, but you didn't. So I did. He's your son and needed to know," Dalton presumed she was talking about the cancer. *"We're at the airport, and will be back in New York by 5 P.M. You need to call him and talk to him. Be a father for once in your life,"* and she hung up.

Dalton thought it was typical Lilly to throw that last jab—if boxer's used words instead of their fists Lilly could be the heavyweight champ.

Next message was from his agent in New York...

"Dalton—it's Jonathan Price, just checking in to see if your still doing the book signing in Traverse City, I never heard back from you. If so, I think I'll drive up—I'll be in Detroit for a meeting that weekend. Besides, it's been a while. The book's selling like crazy—it's just amazing. Call me, you got the number, gotta catch a cab," and he hung up.

Dalton looked at the calendar on the wall, he'd forgot about the book signing. He walked into the living room and noticed the ashes from yesterday's fire, an appropriate metaphor he thought as he climbed the stairs of his empty home.

He drew a hot bath, took a handful of pain pills, and opened a fifth of whiskey. Sam came into the bathroom and assumed his position on the wooden stool as Dalton lowered himself into the tub.

Dalton gulped the whiskey, it burned a little and he coughed. He hurt so bad.

Water dripped from the faucet as he soaked in the tub. A spider moved slowly across the wall into a crack in the plaster. Dalton closed his eyes, tried to push the last few days from his mind, and fell asleep in the tub.

He woke up in cool water.

Sam was gone.

Dalton leaned forward and pulled the drain for the tub, and a pain shot up his back that took his breath away.

As the water was draining, Dalton stood up and slipped, he went down, hit the faucet with his face, and gashed open his forehead.

He laid there for a moment in the bottom of the tub, and when he opened his eyes he watched the last of the bloody water swirl and drain.

It took a while, but he finally got up, stepped out of the bathtub, knocking the fifth of whiskey off the edge of the tub, and it broke on the tile floor. He stepped down on wet tile and broken glass and cut his foot—but was too numb on pain pills and booze to feel it. As he reached for a towel to wipe the blood from his forehead and eyes—he fell again. He slowly stood back up, wrapped himself in a towel, and staggered down the hall leaving a blood-smeared footprint across the wood floor. Dalton passed out in bed while holding the corner of the towel to his bloody forehead.

He woke up when he heard the phone ringing, opened his eyes and sat up slowly. He looked at the clock, it was 8:30 A.M. He still had his towel wrapped around him from the night before, and when he put his feet on the cold floor he realized he must have cut his foot at some point, then noticed the blood on the floor. The telephone stopped ringing and the answering machine went off. He could hear a muffled voice from downstairs, but wasn't sure who it was, didn't really care.

It took a bit to stand up and make his way to the bathroom where he sat on the toilet and urinated a little in pain. He sat there for a little longer trying to remember exactly what happened the night before. Then he stood up in front of the sink leaning on the counter, he looked terrible with dried blood all over his face. He cleaned up with a warm washcloth, and went back to his bedroom, got dressed, then went downstairs, and called Meg.

"Hello?" Meg said.

"Meg," said Dalton with pain in his voice, "I need some help over here."

"I'll be right there."

Thirty-eight

Meg came through the back door and found Dalton sitting in the living room in his chair. When she saw the gash in his head she got scared.

"*Oh my lord Dalton!* Are you all right?"

"I'm all right. I need stitches though."

"What happened?"

"I slipped in the tub."

"Oh my god, let's go—I'll drive."

Hands gripping the wheel, Meg went fast into town. As they sped down Main Street Angie Bartlett and Billy were coming out of the Food Market and saw them drive by, and that Dalton was holding his head.

"Mom, that was Mr. Jones," Billy said, "was he okay?" Angie watched as they sped down the street.

"I don't know," Angie said.

Meg and Dalton arrived at the Doctors office, and the nurses got him in right away when they saw his head. A young nurse cleaned up the head wound, and gave him a shot in the forehead above his eye, and in his foot—then they began to stitch him up.

Aaron came in and asked Dalton twenty questions, and when he found out that Dalton was drinking while on the pain medication he read him the riot act.

Aaron explained to Meg that where the cancer had metastasized to the bone, pelvis, and spine this amount of pain was normal. He gave Dalton several options for pain relief, and wrote some new prescriptions.

"Now be careful with this stuff, and if you have anything to drink with this it could possibly make you sick, or intensify the effect of the alcohol, like you'd had three or four times the amount you actually drank.

"Could it kill me?" Dalton asked. Aaron didn't reply.

After Aaron inspected Dalton's stitches he asked Meg to step out into the hall. He explained to her about Hospice, and that she didn't need to struggle with Dalton all alone, and when it begins to get difficult she needs to call him right away.

"Meg, at this stage without treatment Dalton will decline very quickly. I'll do everything I possibly can do to keep him comfortable for the time he has left."

Meg began to cry, and Aaron gave her a hug.

"Please call me if you need anything. Call here, or at home—all right?"

"I will. Thank you Aaron."

Thirty-nine

Meg took Dalton home, and insisted that he stay in bed. He was feeling terrible and didn't object. He spent most of the morning watching the tall pines outside the window sway in the breeze. Occasionally he'd doze off.

That afternoon as Meg was buzzing around the kitchen, Angie and Billy knocked on the back door. Hank barked once and stood up. Meg opened the door, and was surprised.

"Hello Mrs. Stevens,' Angie said, "I don't mean to pry, but we saw you with Dalton this morning going through town… is everything all right?"

"Oh you two come in from the cold," Meg said. "Hello there young man," she said to Billy, "And please dear, call me Meg." Angie and Billy came inside, and Billy kicked off his boots. "Can I get you anything? Would you like some cookies and milk?"

"Sure!" Billy said

"Billy," Angie said in a hushed voice.

"It's okay honey, if he don't eat them I will, you know. Would you like some hot tea—or coffee?"

"No thank you," Angie said.

"Are you sure, I was just about to pour a cup of tea for myself," Meg said.

"Well, sure," Angie said. "Is Dalton here?"

"He is," Meg said, setting milk and cookies on the table for Billy, then she poured the steaming hot water into the mugs over the tea bags, and sat down at the table. "Dalton fell last night and hit his head, and he had to get a few stitches this morning."

"Is he okay?" Angie asked.

"Oh, it will heal, but Dalton has more worries than that. I guess I can tell you—Dr. Mackenzie told Dalton that he's got cancer. It's pretty bad."

"Has he started any treatment?" Angie asked. Meg shook her head no, and removed her tea bag, squeezed out the excess water, and put it on a small saucer in the middle of the table.

"He's decided not to do anything. It's spread to the bone and all over, his prostate, pelvis, all over. He's got some pain medication to help so he's a little more comfortable—he's been trying to deal with the pain till now, having a little whiskey here and there, and a prescribed painkiller. The new pain meds seem to be helping more, he's slept most of today away. I think Charlie's funeral, and having the family around plum wore him out," Meg said as she wiped a tear from the corner of her eye.

"I had no idea," Angie said.

"What's wrong mom?" Billy asked.

"Mr. Jones is real sick."

"Is he gonna die?" Billy asked. Angie looked at Meg and hesitated, wanting to say no and that everything was going to be all right, but she knew it wasn't.

"Yes," she said softly. "He's very sick and is going to die."

Big tears rolled down Meg's face, and she turned her head. "Meg, can we see him?"

"Oh sure," Meg said. "He sure speaks well of you two—he's very fond of you both." Meg led them upstairs. It was the first time Angie had been up theses steps in years, it was like walking backwards in time, when she used to sneak up to Dan's room when they were in high school. So many memories of time spent. She felt flush and hung on to Billy who was in front of her. Meg knocked on Dalton's half open bedroom door.

"Dalton—you have visitors," she said, and led them in. Dalton sat up a little, looking groggy. "I'll be downstairs if you need me," and

Meg hurried back down to the kitchen.

"Hi," Angie said.

"Hi there," Dalton said attempting to sit up, "what brings you two out here?"

"We saw you and Meg driving through town this morning," Angie said stepping closer to the bed, "and just kind of had this feeling, I wanted to come and check on you."

"Oh," Dalton said. "Well, I'm fine."

"Are you gonna die?" Billy asked, and there was an awkward silence. Dalton was caught off guard, and looked at Angie. Her eyes gave it all away. He looked back down at Billy.

"Yes," he said, "I am Billy. I'm pretty sick."

"Can I catch it?" Billy asked. Angie looked sympathetic, and Dalton slightly grinned.

"No, you can't catch this," Dalton said. Billy didn't say anything, but stepped up to the foot of the bed to pet old Sam.

"He seems to like you," Dalton said, and Billy smiled. Dalton looked back at Angie, "So you talked to Meg. She never could keep a secret."

"I'm glad she told us," Angie said.

"Well, I would've told you sooner or later," said Dalton.

"I'm sorry about the phone call a couple nights ago," Angie said. "I shouldn't have called."

"Oh hell, don't worry about that," Dalton said. "Did he come back and talk to you before he left town?"

"No," Angie said.

"I'm sorry," Dalton said.

"It's all right," Angie said.

Billy continued to rub Sam's belly.

"I'm having a book signing in Traverse City in a couple days," Dalton said, "At the big book store downtown, if you want to come."

"Are you feeling up to it?"

"Meg doesn't think so, but I committed to this, so I'm doing it.

"Your book got a good review in the Detroit paper," Angie said.

"Then it's the first good review they've given me in thirty years," Dalton said, and Angie laughed.

"Well, we'll try to go. It depends a lot on work and homework."

"Understood," Dalton said. "Even if you don't go, I could probably sign a copy for you."

"That sounds good," Angie smiled. "Well, we better go, let you rest."

"Thanks for stopping by Billy," Dalton said. "I guess old Sam needed some attention." Billy smiled, they said goodbye, and Sam followed them out of the room when they left. Dalton listened as they made their way down the stairs, said goodbye to Meg, and out the back door.

Dalton sat there for a while, then climbed out of bed, and limped down stairs.

"What are you doing up?" Meg said as she stirred a boiling pot on the stove.

"I have to make a phone call," said Dalton. He flipped through his little address book and dialed the number of his lawyer friend, George Ashton. Meg listened with one ear.

"George?—It's Dalton Jones. Yes, I'm fine. Well… no I'm not. I have a cancer." He paused. "George I want you to come out to the house, I need to make some changes to my will, and a few other things—tomorrow will be fine—I'll see you then. Thanks George," and he hung up the phone.

Meg looked over her shoulder at Dalton wondering what he was up to, and went back to stirring.

Dalton went back to bed and slept on and off till supper, then came down stairs and ate with Meg, then back to bed. His new wound on his forehead ached, and was a distraction to the rest of his ailments. He went down the hall to the bathroom and took his pain medication. He thought about drinking some whiskey, but changed his mind, and limped back to bed.

Forty

When Dalton woke up the alarm clock was flashing 4:35 A.M. He lay there for a while before moving. He walked to the bathroom in his shorts and tee-shirt, attempted to urinate. He took his pills, and wished he could take a bath—but couldn't until those stitches were out. Instead, he went quietly downstairs, not wanting to wake Meg, and made coffee.

As Dalton poured hot coffee into a mug he saw they got another foot of snow overnight. He flipped the switch for the overhead light in the kitchen, sat down at the table, and tried not to think about how bad he felt. He took a deep breath, and knew dying wasn't going to be easy.

He sipped his coffee and wrote in his journal for about an hour and a half before Meg woke up. Dalton wrote about Dan and his regret as to how their time together turned sour, and how much he loved his son, and how perhaps he took his own fears and frustration out on Dan that night.

Dalton wrote that he saw Dan as such a talented young man, with so much potential—all the opportunities life has to offer him were at his fingertips. Dalton wanted him to take advantage of it all, and not to waste as much time as he did; but Dalton didn't know how to express something like that without seeming like he was forcing his dreams on Dan.

He wondered what Dan's dreams were, and what he saw himself doing in the years to come. Dalton realized it didn't really matter what Dan ended up doing as long as he was happy, and content with this life. Dalton hoped that as time passed that Dan could learn from his old man's mistakes and lead a more positive productive life.

Dalton had spent most of his life recording his thoughts, ideas, and imaginings—when he should of spent more of it living.

If only he could go back and live it all again and to make the right choices—take a sober walk along the beach with his family, without picking a fight with his wife, or brooding. To be able to play with his son and tell him how proud he was of him. Dalton stopped writing and looked around the kitchen and imagined children playing in these empty rooms, laughing, saying 'I love you Dad,' and the house would be warm and full of life instead of this dark old drafty place.

It was so quiet.

He could hear the wind outside and the waves lapping against the shore on the bay. Everything else was still, like death. In many ways this house, and Dalton had been dead for a long time.

He'd had so many opportunities to make something of this life, other than being a writer, and he let it all pass by. Everyday he woke up sober, and choose to take another drink. When he did sober up, he kept himself hidden away out on this peninsula, and only truly lived through his writing, and his characters. Back then it seemed like all he needed, but today, faced with the end, he knew it wasn't enough. Now death hung over him like a heavy shroud, and it was too late.

Meg got up around 6:45 A.M. made breakfast and cleaned up. Dalton sat in his chair in the living room, watching the clock, and drifted off to sleep.

Around 8:30 A.M. George Ashton arrived. Meg let him in and gave him a hug. She'd known George for years; he'd handled all her fathers business when he passed away. She took his coat and poured him a cup of coffee, then took him into the living room where Dalton was sleeping in his chair.

"His medications are making him sleep a lot more," Meg said. "Dalton," she touched his shoulder and he woke up suddenly. "George is here." Dalton stirred and looked over his shoulder.

"Oh, hello George," they shook hands. "Thanks for coming out."

"No problem," George said, and sat down on the end of the couch near Dalton's chair. He was startled by the gash on Dalton's forehead.

"What did you do to your head Dalton?"

"Oh, I took a little spill the other night."

"Looks like it hurts."

"A little bit," Dalton said touching the stitches with his fingers.

"If you boys need anything let me know," Meg said and went back in the kitchen.

"So what can I do for you?" George said.

"I'm dying," said Dalton. "I want to change my will." George knew Dalton well, and doing business with him had always been direct and to the point.

"Alright," said George, pulling out a pad of legal paper and pen.

"I want Meg to have enough money that she doesn't have to worry about anything; she may need special care someday, and I don't ever want her to have to worry about the financial side of things," Dalton said.

"Next, I'd like to pay off my son, Dan, with the sum that we discussed in the past. I want this house to go to him. At some point I'd like to think he'd want to come home."

George was taking notes and nodding his head.

"Now here's what is a little different," Dalton continued, "You know Angie Bartlett and her boy Billy?"

"Sure, sure I do," said George.

"I want to set up some kind of a trust fund for the boy, something he can't get at till he's a little older, say for college, or something like that—and not where he gets it all at once, slowly over time."

"Okay, we can do that," George said starting to write again.

"Now for Angie, I've been thinking about this, I want you to draw up a check, and I wrote some numbers down here for you," Dalton took a piece of paper out of his shirt pocket and handed it to George.

George looked a little startled when he saw how much Dalton wanted it for. "I want a check in Angie's name, and if there isn't enough cash for that amount take some of it out of Dan's share."

"Alright," George said.

"That's it—everything else stays the same. Can you think of anything I missed?"

"No—not yet. I'll go interpret all this into some legal documents and be back out next week for you to sign."

"Good," Dalton said. "The sooner the better, if you know what I mean."

"Understood," George said. Meg came in the room and warmed up George's coffee.

"George, are you hungry?"

"Oh no, Meg—I'm fine."

"God damnit George," Dalton said, "I heard your stomach growling, you need to eat."

"Well," George said.

"How do you like your eggs?" Meg asked.

"Poached, I guess," George said, and Meg headed back to the kitchen with a purpose. She knew Dalton already ate, but she'd try to feed him again. George smiled and sipped his coffee.

"Everyone needs someone like her," George said.

"She's available," said Dalton.

"I'll keep that in mind," George said. He sipped his coffee and Hank came in and leaned up against George's leg, looking for a scratch, or a pat on the head.

Dalton looked out the window and said, "So how about all this god damn snow?"

Forty-one

The next day Meg was rushing around the house, and Dalton was upstairs getting dressed. He put on a pair of jeans, a white dress shirt, and a dark blue jacket. He found some blue socks and dress shoes that needed polished.

Meg was rushing up and down the hall, from her room to the bathroom.

"I still don't think you should go to this," she yelled.

"I'm going," Dalton yelled back.

"You need your rest," she said.

"*Jesus* Meg!" Dalton growled. "I'll be dead soon. I'll get all kinds of rest then. Besides, I said I'd do this, and I'm going to. I *want* to do this."

"It's just not like you to want to go to a book signing," Meg said.

"Knowing I won't ever have to do it again makes it seem almost fun."

Dalton was putting on his jacket as Meg stepped into the room, and he smiled at her.

"You look real nice," he said. Meg got embarrassed.

"Oh this old thing, I'm surprised it even fits," she said. "Are you sure you want to do this?"

"*Yes*," Dalton said. "I want to do this."

"Okay, you know I'm just worried about you."

"I know. Don't be, I can do this."

"Okay, lets go then," she said. Dalton held out his hand and took hers, and they headed downstairs.

Meg drove Dalton to Traverse city to the big bookstore. They parked and walked in through the front door. Dalton went up to the cash register and told the young girl that he was there for the book signing. Without looking up she said, "It's going to take place in the back, and there's already a line forming,— but there are a lot of seats and I'm sure you will make it in."

"I hope I make it in, I'm the author young lady."

She turned bright red and stopped what she was doing. Now Dalton had her undivided attention.

"Oh, umm, Mr. Jones! Let me call my manager, she's waiting for you. The girl fumbled with the phone and called the manager, who quickly came rushing out, a heavyset woman in a tight black dress. Dalton thought she was a pretty woman.

"Mr. Jones!," she said smiling, smelling like cigarettes, "what a pleasure it is to have you here, will you come with me?" she lead them back to her office and offered them water or coffee.

"Do you have a cup with ice?" Dalton asked. She seemed perplexed.

"Well, yes, I suppose I can get that." So she brought Meg some coffee, and Dalton a cup with ice. He pulled a small flask from his pocket, opened it, and poured whiskey over the ice.

"This is all right, isn't it?" Dalton asked.

"Oh, certainly," she said. "I dabble in the arts as well, you know, and like to have the occasional glass of wine to unwind, get the creative juices flowing."

"Exactly," Dalton said.

"Mr. Jones," she said leaning forward on her elbows and resting her breasts on the desk, "I just loved your new book, it might be my favorite of them all." Dalton put the flask back in his inside jacket pocket, and Meg sipped her coffee from a paper cup.

"Thank you," Dalton said. "What did you like about it?"

"Oh my gosh, everything," she said gesturing with her hands. "The way you captured the loneliness of the main character, and his desire to do something good before he dies—it was perfect. I've read all your books, and when I heard that you were killing your *star* protagonist, I was *shocked*! Upset! But you did it in such a perfect way, it was beautiful, I cried!" she said.

Dalton took a drink, the ice in his cup was beginning to melt.

"Well thank you, that's quite a compliment," he said. She leaned back in her chair and he took another drink.

"Your work, it's so meaningful—it just fills me up. You have an amazing gift," she said. Meg looked over and noticed Dalton looking glassy eyed from the whiskey he was drinking.

The manager's phone rang and she excused herself for a moment, and left the room. "Handsome woman," Dalton said.

"You be careful with that whiskey—you're on a lot of medicine."

"I'm okay Meg, really."

"Like I said, be careful with the whiskey."

The manager went to the gathering area, where they'd opened up the seating and people were starting to shuffle in. People had brought with them copies of the new book, one guy had bought fifteen copies, and others brought their old favorites.

The room was filling up quickly, and it wouldn't be long before they would run out of seats. The manager stood there practically hugging herself with excitement, she loved these events, and it'd been a while since they'd had a turn out quite like this.

One of her young employees came up to her and told her there was a man here to see Mr. Jones.

"He said his name was Jonathan Price, Mr. Jones' agent," the young girl said.

The manager went to Jonathan, who was a tall good-looking man, and very well dressed. They shook hands, and she led him back to her office.

"Quite a turn out," Jonathan said looking at the crowd.

"Isn't it wonderful," she said. "We just love Mr. Jones." When they entered the office Dalton was sipping his whiskey. "Mr. Jones, I believe you know this man?" Dalton looked up.

"Hello Jonathan!" he said, slowly standing up and shook his hand.

"Dalton. What happened to your head?"

"Oh, I had a little fall, least of my worries. This is my sister Meg Stevens."

"Hello Ma'am," Jonathan said and they shook hands.

"If you will excuse me," the manager said, and she stepped out again.

"You have a full house,' Jonathan said. "Its like the crowds you draw in Manhattan—this is great!" Dalton smiled and looked over at Meg, sipping her coffee, and smoothing out her dress.

"Are you going to read an excerpt from the book?"

"Yeah," Dalton said casually. "I have a couple things I want to read, and say."

"Good, you know what these are all about, I'm sure you'll do great," Jonathan said.

"Jonathan, I have to tell you something," Dalton said as Jonathan sat on the corner of the manager's desk. "I have cancer. It's terminal. I don't have much longer."

Jonathan was half grinning thinking this was some kind of joke; then he noticed that Dalton had lost weight and was looking frailer than the last time he saw him.

"You're serious?"

"Yes," Dalton said, and Meg looked down into her lap.

"Terminal?" Jonathan asked.

"Yes," said Dalton. "This may be the last time I see you."

"Are you serious?" Jonathan said, disbelieving.

"I know we haven't worked together all that long, but I want you to know you've been a damn good agent to work with," Dalton said.

"Thank you," Jonathan said. "I don't know what to say."

"You don't have to say anything. It's a shitty thing this cancer. It snuck up on me and bit me in the ass." There was a long pause in the room. Dalton took another sip of whiskey and Jonathan starred at the floor. "I'm glad you came tonight," Dalton said.

"Me too," Jonathan said. "How are you feeling?"

"Like hell. But I promise not to die out there in front of everyone."

"Oh god Dalton," Meg said. Dalton pulled the flask out of his coat pocket, took off the cap and refreshed his drink, then handed the flask to Jonathan.

"Here, take a drink and enjoy the show." Jonathan took the flask, paused, then tipped the flask back, swallowed, and coughed.

"Oh my god!" he said and coughed again, and handed it back to Dalton.

"Meg?" Dalton said, holding up the flask.

"Oh heavens no!" she said and sipped her coffee.

"Sure?" Dalton said with a grin.

"Oh," she hesitated and looked to see if Jonathan had recovered, "why not," and she took the flask and tipped it back. She wiped her lips and laughed. Dalton laughed as well, that was the first time he'd seen his sister take a drink in thirty years. They were all laughing when the manager came back into the room.

"Sounds like there is a party going on in here!" she said. "I think we're about ready for you Mr. Jones—are you ready?"

"I'm ready," Dalton said. He stood up and pulled his pants up a little. They all followed the manager out and down the hall. Dalton could hear the excited crowd, and the hush when someone went on stage to test the microphone. They all stepped out into the room, and before Dalton could even step onto the low stage the crowd stood and applauded him, and the manager was all smiles and stepped up to the microphone at the podium.

"Ladies and gentlemen, it is with *great pleasure*, I would like to introduce to you one of northern Michigan's *treasures*, Mr. Dalton Jones." The crowd applauded him again as he stepped up to the microphone. Meg and Jonathan had stepped off to the side and found seats reserved for them. Dalton took another sip of his drink and set it on the table next to the podium, then cleared his throat.

"Good evening," he said as the crowd began to quiet down. Dalton scanned the crowd, and noticed Angie and Billy in the very back of the room. He was pleased to see them.

Dalton was aware that this was the last time he'd ever be before a crowd like this, and he wanted to take everything in. All these people gave up their time for him—it was awkward, and humbling. All these faces smiling, a cough, and a baby cried off in the corner.

"I wanted to read to you a passage from my latest book, but I have a few things I want to say first. This will be my last public appearance." The crowd began a nervous chatter, and a few pictures were taken. "I have cancer." There were a few gasps in the crowd, shocked uncomfortable expressions. The manager stood off to the side with her hand over her mouth. "It's terminal," Dalton said.

A woman in the front row started to cry.

"So, *in lieu* of that news, lets try to have a good time. This evening is as special to me as it is for all of you. I will sign some autographs, as many as I can. I'd like to say hello to everyone."

The crowd started to applaud again, and then everyone stood up.

"Please, thank you—thank you," and the room quieted down to a hush again. "I have a few passages from the new book I'd like to read. This first one is from chapter one, when we we're climbing back into our protagonist's brain for the first time after all these years...

I've been down for the better part of the decade. Feeling despair, and sadness. Friends are worried, I don't know what to tell them, and they think I'm keeping something from them, but its nothing more than just a dream.

I dreamt of her again last night...' Her being the leading lady from the first novel." Dalton said, and continued, "'*I dreamt of her last night. I held her close, and she was perfect and beautiful. I have everything in life, but none of it means anything to me. I'm searching for something but I don't know where to look. I just want the sadness to go away and to discover happiness again.*

I don't need much, just a quiet place that isn't cluttered, a place to think and create. She would be there, and we would talk about all things. She'd listen to me, and I would listen to her—and we'd have respect, admiration, and trust. I want to make a difference in peoples' lives, and to be happy, to laugh some everyday. I want my life to be full of creativity, and positive energy. I want to be closer to God. I don't want to struggle anymore, and I want to surround myself with people who are happy, who love themselves and this life.

I want to have more time for the things that are important to me. My art and creative expression is my path to understanding what this life has been all about. I just want to be happier, and to laugh—to feel alive and to be excited about life again. There is so much to do, and I want to take advantage of everything while I can."

Dalton paused and took another drink. You could've heard a pen drop in the room.

The woman in the front row was still crying.

He went on…

"As I said, I dreamt of her last night. She haunts me. I've attempted to contact her, but she wouldn't respond. It would be good to hear from her once in a while, to know she's happy. If she were hurt, or dead—I would never know. Every once in a while I search for her, an announcement, a marriage, a baby, anything—but nothing.

To separate myself from the situation was nearly impossible, and my story went on leaving these unwritten chapters, like open wounds unable to heal. I think about her and wonder where she is, happy, lonely, content, I just don't know.

Years ago, after several drunken letters, she responded. She said…

'I feel for you and your situation, I have moved on. I wish for your freedom. Life brings us many winding roads, you must travel yours, and I mine. Please do not contact me again.'

When I read that letter I let go. In many ways her words set me free, and brought me peace. I resumed my life, or built a new one.

So much time has passed, and now it's only this vague reoccurring dream where I hold her close and she is perfect and beautiful."

Dalton paused and looked up.

"Thank you," he said and closed the book.

The room broke into applause again, a few people whistled and hollered something from the back of the room. They wanted more, and not for this to be the end.

Dalton took another drink and held up his hand, and they quieted down. "I don't have anything else planned to read this evening, but I'd like to answer questions before I start signing autographs—and hands started to go up immediately. He called on a man in the front row.

"Did you base the protagonist after yourself?"

"Good question," Dalton said. "I think, in some respects, yes. But the original inspiration for the character came from my first cousin—his name was Edward.

In many ways, I think this character has allowed me to maintain the relationship I lost with my cousin's death. It was a tragic and sudden death, and I never had closure.

I think through all my stories and adventures with this character, in many ways I've been attempting to deal with my cousin's suicide. In some ways I've been successful, others I have not. There will always be some lingering residue from that loss. I can say with the conclusion of this character's life in this novel, I have put aspects of my long standing grief to rest."

The crowd was silent. For those who had followed Dalton's career knew that was probably the longest, most heartfelt response he'd ever given.

He pointed to a young woman in the fifth row.

"Do you have any advice for a young writer?" she asked.

Dalton smiled.

"Yes," he said. "I recently read a statement by the author Natalie Goldberg that I liked, she said that as writers, we live twice, like a cow that eats its food once, and then regurgitates it to chew and digest it again. We all have a second chance at biting into our experience and examining it. Our lives will not last forever, and there isn't time to think 'someday I'll write that short story, or poem,' sit down and put your pen to paper, and begin to write. Wasn't it Buddha who said the trouble is, you think you have time." The young woman in the audience smiled. "How about you sir?" Dalton pointed to a tall skinny man about his age.

The man stood up slowly and asked, "Do you believe in God?"

"Oh no," Meg whispered to Jonathan, she had no idea how Dalton was going to respond. In all the years, all the book signings, and all the questions, Dalton had never been asked this before. He stood silent for a moment before he answered.

"Yes," Dalton said, "I do—but maybe not in a practical sense. I've never felt like I needed a church to have a relationship with God. Most of my life I've struggled, seeking God, but what I never realized until my later years was that God was always there, all around me, everywhere, in everything, all the time.

When I was young I couldn't recognize God in the face of my child. I couldn't hear God's voice in the lapping waves upon the lake shore. I couldn't feel God's presence as I walked in the sun. I was naive. But today, being close to the end, I'm very aware of these things. I'm aware of this presence in every moment.

One of the great questions in my life is why we have to suffer so. This cancer that I have is painful, and I wonder after all these years of suffering, what purpose does it serve for me to die this meaningless, painful death? I know this is more of an answer than you bargained for, but it's the truth I've been grappling with.

So do I believe in God? Yes." Dalton said. "Do I understand God? No. Do I have any final thoughts on my life? Mostly confusion, unanswered questions, and a longing for more time," Dalton said.

The room was silent.

"Speaking of time, I better sign some books. Thank you everyone," he said, and stepped away from the podium. There was an applause again, Dalton just stood there and absorbed it, and smiled.

The bookstore manager and her staff organize a line, and had Dalton sit down at the big wooden table next to the podium. They gave him a pile of markers, water, and another cup with ice.

The room was a buzz. Dalton was tired, but felt strongly about doing this. He signed autographs for over an hour, and was shaking hands, and posing for pictures.

Dalton signed hundreds of books and the line was down to the last thirty people or so, everyone was still waiting patiently. They all wanted to share something with him, a story, a thought, a smile. Dalton was moved, and wished he'd been more receptive to his fans years ago. One book after another slid in front of him and

Dalton personalized every book. In total he signed three hundred and twenty books, and when finished, he shook the managers hand, and posed for a picture with some of the staff.

He was exhausted when Angie and Billy came up to him. Angie hugged Dalton.

"You were wonderful tonight," she said. Dalton smiled, and touched Billy on the shoulder, and was surprised when Billy took his hand, looked up and smiled.

"Dalton," Jonathan said, "I have to go—I have a meeting in Detroit in the morning. Thank you, for everything Dalton. I'll be in touch soon. I feel like I should say..."

"It's alright Jonathan." The two men shook hands.

"Thank you too," Dalton said, and Jonathan left.

Dalton turned back to Angie. Meg was there now, and she took Dalton by the elbow and said it was time to go.

Meg drove Dalton home. It was clear night and the moon reflected off Grand Traverse Bay. She steered the car along M-22 north, Dalton was silent as he stared out the window watching the moon, rocks, and the trees along the shore. On they went through Bingham, Suttons Bay, Peshawbesttown, Omena, then into Northport.

"You need anything in town," Meg asked. They were the first words spoken the entire drive.

"No. I don't think so," Dalton said, slouching in the passengers seat still looking out the window as they drove passed the Grandview.

"I need to go see Fred Anderson over at the funeral home tomorrow," Dalton said. "I'll do that myself, you don't have to go."

Meg was about to protest, but then agreed. She turned the old truck onto CR-629, heading further north towards the lighthouse, towards Cathead Bay, and home.

Forty-two

In a suburb in Midland, Elizabeth Wharton poured herself a mug of coffee and sat down at the kitchen table with the morning newspaper. It was a beautiful morning, bright blue sky and a few inches of fresh snow. She unfolded the newspaper and turned to the arts section, she sipped her coffee while scanning the articles. She turned to the next page and saw the headline '*Final Appearance for Michigan Author, Dalton Jones.*'

Elizabeth set her coffee mug down, and glanced up and down the hall, her husband Roger was still in the shower. She flattened the newspaper in front of her and read the article.

When she finished she sat there for a moment looking at the photo of Dalton standing at the podium. He looked so old. There was a flood of memory and emotion, and Elizabeth felt sad, and so alone. She never told her husband about her relationship with Dalton—she never felt like she needed to. Roger knew she was married before, and that her husband had taken his own life, but never all the extraneous details.

Over the years she avoided anything and everything 'Dalton Jones'—his books, that section of the bookstore, his name if brought up in conversation, everything. Part of her felt like she was keeping a secret from Roger, but whenever she had gotten close to telling him, she backed away. It was a part of her past that was long since gone, and so unnecessary to drudge up.

She thought about her lecture in Traverse City, and that Dalton had been there. She wondered what they would've said to one another if he would have approached her. She was relieved he didn't. She wondered if he'd come to tell her about the cancer, maybe.

Elizabeth leaned back in her chair and thought about the last few times she'd seen Dalton, Grand Central Station, his father's funeral, walking along the shore to the light house, the night in the hotel…

"Where are you at?" Roger said and he walked through the kitchen towards the coffee pot, hair still wet from the shower.

Elizabeth quickly folded the newspaper over, covering the article.

"Oh, I was just thinking about everything I have to do today, that's all," she lied. Roger nodded and poured himself coffee, and walked back into the other room.

Elizabeth stood up and took that section of the paper and put it in the recycle bin under the desk, then was straightening the remaining paper on the table as Roger walked back into the kitchen.

"So what's first on your list of things to do?" He asked. Elizabeth had no idea, everything she was thinking about before she read that article was gone, it took her a few moments to recover. "Are you sure your all right honey?" Roger asked concerned.

"I'm fine," she said. "I have a little head ache, that's all." He stepped close to her and kissed her, and smiled.

"Why don't you go lay down for a while if your not feeling well, I'm sure everything else can wait," Roger said.

"Your right," Elizabeth said. Roger hugged her.

"I have to run to the drugstore to pick up my prescription, I'll be right back," he said. "You need anything while I'm out?"

"No," Elizabeth said.

She watched him pull out of the driveway.

There was a lost forgotten part of her emerging, she felt as if she could cry. She walked around the house, straightening this, picking up that. She went back to the kitchen and looked out the window over the sink at the fresh snow piled on the branches of winter trees.

Elizabeth closed her eyes and went back in time, to Cathead Bay, to a time when she and Dalton walked the path along the shore, through the pines towards the lighthouse. She did most of the talking, and asked him where he could see himself in sixty years.

Dalton looked around, smiled, and said, "Right here."

Elizabeth laughed, but he didn't.

They shared big thoughts on life as they walked along. The wind was cold, but the sun was warm. The water was blue and the gulls lined the rocky shore.

They walked around the lighthouse, and sat in the old gazebo and talked. Elizabeth could recall how the warm sun felt on her face that day—If there was ever a moment that seemed perfect she thought, it was there.

That evening they met at a little diner that had green and white checkered table cloths. They had an invigorating conversation. Every word he spoke rang through her, his words came so easily for him.

She felt they were so close to the same. He brought her such ease, even though he was in so much turmoil.

That night, at the diner, she said to him "I'm glad I met you Dalton Jones," and he smiled.

They left the diner that night and went together just out of town to a cheap little hotel with a neon light. They checked in, and went to the room together. They made love, and as they lay there entwined, out on Lake Michigan two freighters crossed paths, blowing their deep dreary sighs into the night—acknowledging the others presence, and passed on.

While seeking answers to her questions Elizabeth only came across more complexities, layers, and new questions. She wondered if the love she felt for Dalton was true. There were so many layers throughout their lives that overlapped and caused confusion.

In the early hours of the morning they made love again. Afterwards, as they lie there in the dark, Dalton told her that Lily was pregnant, and Elizabeth recoiled.

He told her that Lilly's pregnancy had been their last desperate attempt to save their marriage.

Elizabeth remembered Dalton telling her that he loved her, and that he had loved her since before she married Edward, and that he didn't want to let anything come between them ever again.

"What about Lilly?" Elizabeth asked, but Dalton didn't know what to say. He tried to kiss her again, but she pushed him away.

"Lilly's pregnant," she said. They both laid there in silence.

Eventually Dalton fell asleep, and Elizabeth slipped out of bed and away from the hotel. She drove home to Edward. It was that night Edward confronted her about the letters he'd found from Dalton, and he hit her. Two days later Edward hung himself in their garage. The aftermath, and the horrible day of the funeral. Seven months later Dalton and Lilly's son was born.

Elizabeth thought about the last time she saw Dalton, and all the years that had passed and his absence from her life. All the winding roads she'd taken since then.

She thought about Edward. She wanted to weep for him—for herself—and for Dalton.

Roger stepped in through the back door and startled Elizabeth.

"I thought you were going to lay down," he said.

"I guess I got a little side tracked," she said. He sat his prescription down on the counter top and went to her. They embraced.

"Are you sure your all right?" he asked.

"Yes," she said. "I just need you to hold me for a while."

"Alright," he said.

"Roger... I love you so much. You truly are the best thing in my life," Elizabeth said, attempting to push Dalton from her thoughts.

She loved Roger. She couldn't go back there to the past again. It was such an unsettled, unhappy time in her life, full of regret and pain. It would do her no good to remember any more.

Forty-three

That morning Dalton slept in until 8:45 A.M. The painkillers helped him sleep. He got up and took another small dose, didn't shower, dressed, and combed his hair. Meg cooked breakfast, and the kitchen smelled of bacon and coffee. They sat at the table, made small talk, and ate together.

When Dalton finished his food, he took one last swallow of coffee.

"I'm full Meg. Thank you for breakfast." He slid back his chair and got up from the table. "I better get going," he said, and kissed Meg on top of the head. He slowly put on his boots, hat, and went out to the truck. Dalton was surprised at the effort it took to push in the clutch. The engine turned over and started right up, which he was thankful for. He sat there and blasted the defroster till the windshield thawed out.

Fred Anderson's funeral home was just down from the Leelanau Township cemetery, over off Kitchen Road. It took Dalton about twenty minutes to get there, driving slow due to the icy roads. When he pulled up in front of the funeral home, Fred was out front throwing salt on the shoveled walk. Dalton got out of the old truck and, with effort, slammed the door.

"How's business Fred?"

"Can't complain," Fred said. "Saw your big write up in the paper this morning."

"How's that?"

"For your book-signing in Traverse yesterday. You really wowed 'em."

"Oh, they got that out fast," Dalton said.

"It's these computers you know, everything's fast now a days. Sometimes I feel like a man in the wrong time." Fred put down the bag of salt and shook Dalton's hand.

"Suppose you know why I'm here then," Dalton said.

"Well, either you want a haircut, or you're here to do some business."

"Both, if I can get it," Dalton said. "If I pay today do I get the haircut for free?"

"Oh what the hell—I'd rather do it now than later," Fred said.

Dalton followed Fred into the funeral home. They walked through the lobby and into Fred's small office. It was dark, and smelled like cigar smoke. He had a space heater on blowing warm air on the floor under his desk.

"Well Fred," Dalton said, "I don't know exactly how all this works. I don't want anything fancy. I want to be cremated, a simple urn. I don't want a showing, or a big funeral. How much for something like that?"

Fred wrote some numbers down on a sheet of paper and slid the paper across the desk to Dalton.

Dalton looked down at what Fred wrote.

"Holy hell Fred, I don't want a golden urn!"

"Now Dalton," Fred said leaning back in his chair and re-lit the half smoked cigar from the ashtray, "I'm not gouging you." He puffed on the cigar and a big blue ring of smoke encircled his head. "That's the price. I'm sure as hell not giving you a discount—you got more money than most of Leelanau Peninsula."

Dalton leaned back in his chair.

"Haircut still free?"

"You bet."

Forty-four

A while later Dalton left the funeral home a little drunk with a fresh haircut. On his way home he pulled off Kitchen road into the cemetery and parked the truck near the entrance. He sat there for a moment watching two white-tailed deer walking cautiously through the cemetery leaving tracks in the fresh snow. Dalton climbed out of the truck as the deer passed over the hill. The frozen snow crunched beneath his feet as he walked back towards Charlie's grave, and with each deep breath the cold air filled his lungs.

At Charlie's grave a simple granite headstone was now in place. Feeling tired after the short hike across the cemetery, Dalton sat on the corner of the headstone. He looked up to the sky where dark clouds were gathering. A bitter, cold breeze blew from the west. Besides the wind, everything was still and serene.

Dalton thought about Charlie, and felt like there was something he should say here, but all he could hear was Charlie's voice in his head saying *"My world renowned brother-in-law, the writer, who has wrote thousands and thousands of words can't think of a god damn thing to say!"* Dalton grimaced—but nothing specific came to him, just memories and emotions, and Dalton's own fears on what was to come.

Dalton was cold and stood back up, read Charlie's headstone again, then turned and walked a few rows over to where his parents graves were, *Daniel Augustus Jones* and *Emily Margaret Jones*, and next to them was his cousin's grave, *Edward M. Jones.*

Dalton recalled the day they buried Edward—it was the winter of 1963—the black hearse, and the empty sick feeling Dalton had as he helped carry Edward's casket to this grave.

He remembered as they approached the grave-side he stepped on a lump of clay that had rolled off the mound of dirt from the new grave—it stuck to the bottom of his shoe, and when he tried to scrape the clay off in the grass it only smeared across the side and front of his shoe.

Dalton looked across the grave and could still imagine Elizabeth's blank stare, as she sat next to his mother and father, in those cold metal folding chairs. As the old reverend spoke, and members of the local Veterans of Foreign Wars played Taps, Dalton continued to wipe the clay off his shoe in the grass, but it only made it worse, and finally Dalton surrendered himself to be covered in clay. He looked up as the member's of the VFW folded an American flag and presented it to Elizabeth. Then Elizabeth looked up at Dalton with a pained stare, she was in shock. She felt responsible for Edward's death—as did Dalton, they were both consumed with grief, guilt, and anguish—anguish that Dalton carried with him to this very day. He wanted to go to her then, to hold her, to protect her, to take her so far away from all that. Looking back, Dalton knew it was then—that moment—that he truly lost her, and everything that came after was merely attempts for resolution, to carry on with their lives, to shake the awful truth of their affair and the pain they caused Edward.

A cold wind continued to blow, and Dalton noticed the two deer were back, cautiously stepping through the frozen snow. He wondered what those final moments for Edward must have been like. The pain he must have been in, to end his life the way he did—hanging from the rafters of that old garage.

Dalton looked back towards the dark grey clouds that were rolling in from over Lake Michigan; there was another storm coming. He was so cold, and hurt deep inside. Like that clay at the funeral, Dalton had surrendered himself to this cancer. Perhaps the cancer was a manifestation of the unbearable guilt that he'd been consumed with all these years.

Forty-five

After that day Dalton didn't leave the house, and the days all started to run together. He was loosing weight and his appetite. He knew he was declining much faster than expected. His days consisted of the early afternoons, he'd sit and write in his journal for a half an hour or so, then lay back down until suppertime. Meg stayed at the house with him, and if she had to be gone any amount of time she'd call Angie to come and sit with Dalton.

Angie was kind to Dalton, and never made him feel like an old dying man, which he appreciated. With Angie he'd talk about art, poetry, or question her about her photography.

When Aaron Mackenzie came out for a house-call, he increased Dalton's pain medication, and gave Meg more information about when to start Hospice. George Ashton came back, and brought legal documents for Dalton to sign, and left a few copies of the documents and the check Dalton requested in a white envelope next to his bed. Before George left that day, it was a sad goodbye. He was standing next to Dalton's bed,

"We never went on that fishing trip."

"You know what George," Dalton said, "I never liked fishing all that much." George smiled, choking up with tears.

The two old friends shook hands, and George went downstairs where Meg was in the kitchen.

He went to her and hugged her tightly.

"Now Meg, if you need anything at all please call me. Even if you just want to go out for coffee, I'm usually sitting alone over at my place waiting for the phone to ring."

"I will George," Meg said.

"If Dalton needs anything as well, you call me."

"Okay," Meg said, and George hugged her again.

That afternoon the phone rang and Meg picked it up, "Hello?"

"Meg? It's Lilly."

"Oh Lilly," Meg said genuinely happy to hear from her.

"How's he doing?" Lilly asked. Meg choked up, and sat down at the kitchen table to talk.

"Not too good," she said. "It's coming faster than we thought. Lilly, if you or Dan are going to come and see him, you need to come very soon. I don't think..." she started to cry, "I don't think he has too much longer."

"How are you holding up Meg?" Lilly asked.

"Oh, I'm all right, I don't think any of this has really sunk in yet. I'm sure when I go home it will," Meg said.

"Have you been staying there at the house?" Lilly asked.

"Yes," Meg said. "He had a bad fall in the tub, you know, and since then I don't think he wants to be alone. Lilly, will you tell Dan he needs to come home—Dalton will never ask, but he needs to see him.

"I will Meg, I'll call him tonight," Lilly said. "I'll call back in a few days to see how things are going, okay."

"Alright, thanks for calling Lilly," Meg said. "I hope you can make it out too."

"I'll see what I can do," Lilly said.

"Okay. Alright. Goodbye," Meg said.

"Goodbye Meg," Lilly said, and hung up the phone.

Lilly sat there at her dining room table staring out the window overlooking the Hudson River.

She lit a cigarette.

Walter walked into the room adjusting his tie.

"How is he?" Walter asked.

"Not good."

"I wonder if he's made all his arrangements."

"Who knows," said Lilly, "probably not."

"Do you know who's taking care of everything when the time comes?"

"Hell, I don't know Walter!" Lilly snapped. "I'm sure its not *you* so you don't have to worry about it."

She took a long drag off her cigarette.

"You want to go see him, to say goodbye?" Walter asked as Lilly blew smoke into the air and ashed her cigarette.

"I don't know," Lilly said, feeling like all the pressures of life were inflating and about to burst.

"If you want to go I'll understand," Walter said as he put on his suit jacket. "When Joan died, the kids and I were there with her."

Lilly's cigarette smoldered as Walter crossed the room and put his hand on her shoulder.

"I think you need to go," he said.

Forty-six

The days were all beginning to blur together for Dalton, and he slept most of his time away. He wrote in his journal when he could, but it was less and less. Meg was bringing most of his meals up to his room, and they would eat together there.

On this particular afternoon she quietly carried a tray with potato soup, and warm bread into the room, assuming Dalton was asleep.

"What's for lunch?" Dalton said.

"Oh, I thought you were asleep," said Meg.

"No, just laying here. Watching the trees. Thinking."

Meg moved around towards the head of the bed and sat in the rocking chair, and looked out the same window as Dalton.

"Remember when Daddy wanted to cut all the trees down so he'd have a better view of the lake from here," Meg said.

"Yeah. Mother put a stop to that one real quick."

"I think once Daddy thought about it, he knew she was right. Can you imagine how bad the wind would be without those trees," Meg said.

The sun shone through the pines, and as the wind blew, shadows danced across the room. Meg leaned back and shut her eyes. Dalton watched her rock slowly in the rocking chair.

"Meg, there is something I have to tell you."

She opened her eyes and stopped rocking.

"Yes?" she said. "Are you all right?"

"I should've told you this a long time ago, but I never could.

I figured you'd hate me, and... I... I've always needed you so much."

"What is it Dalton?" Meg said leaning forward.

"Meg... years ago, Elizabeth and I..."

"Dalton," Meg abruptly interrupted, "I already know."

"What?"

"I've known for years what happened between you two," Meg said.

"You have?"

"Yes," said Meg. Tears welled up in her eyes.

"How? You never said anything..."

"Elizabeth told me. After she left here, after Edward died. She wrote to me, and told me everything. She asked me to never say anything, and I never did."

"You've known all these years?" said Dalton.

Meg leaned even closer and took Dalton's hand.

"Yes."

Dalton closed his eyes.

"I was so wrong Meg, for what I did. I pursued her."

"Dalton, you loved her. You loved her since we were kids. Why punish yourself for something you felt."

"But she was married to Edward."

"And they were having troubles, and she went to you. She knew you loved her. She was scared and alone Dalton."

"I was still wrong."

"Dalton, even if you didn't do what you did, it wouldn't have changed anything. Edward was never the same once he came back from the war. He was depressed, and mean, and drinking.

I don't know if you even know this, but he didn't just hit Elizabeth the one time, he hit her a lot towards the end. She would leave, and Edward would show up at our place, drunk, crying, and plead for us to find her and bring her home. Well, she'd go home, and it would happen all over again.

When he found your letters, it was just one more excuse to beat her up again. If it wasn't that, it would have been something else. Edward was so angry, bad things happened to him in Korea.

I don't know what, he never said, but it changed him, and he was never the same. I always hoped, with time, things might get better. But looking back, I don't think they ever would've.

Elizabeth and Edward were never right for one another. She was so young, and I think just caught up in the idea of getting married, and being married. They didn't even really know one another, not the way a married couple should. They never had a solid foundation to build upon."

"But I slept with my cousin's wife—I was wrong."

"And how you've punished yourself, Dalton."

"I was wrong," Dalton said again.

"You made a poor choice. You loved her, didn't you?"

"I thought so."

"If only we all followed our hearts."

"No..."

"Dalton, Edward would have *done* what he *did* one way or another. You didn't kill him. He killed himself, *do you hear me*, he killed himself. He made that choice, and it was awful. Some people just can't handle this world, this life. He couldn't, his mother couldn't after his Daddy died—that's why he came to live with us. Edward never had anything solid in his life until Mother and Daddy took him in. In a lot of ways it was already too late. Do you understand what I'm saying?"

"I do. It's just... I've felt so bad, for so long."

"*Look at me*," Meg said with big tears rolling down her cheeks. Dalton opened his eyes and looked at his sister. "*It's not your fault*. I never blamed you, or Elizabeth for what Edward did. I love you Dalton."

Dalton squeezed Meg's hand, and closed his eyes tightly—forcing back the tears, "I love you Meg."

Forty-seven

The next morning Angie and Billy showed up and brought a big lunch, some groceries Meg needed, and Dalton's prescriptions.

"Oh honey, you didn't have to bring lunch," Meg said.

"We wanted to."

"Well, thank you."

"How's he doing?" Angie asked.

"About the same. He's awake if you want to go up."

Meg put the groceries away, and Angie and Billy went upstairs, Hank followed. Angie knocked lightly on Dalton's bedroom door before they stepped into the room. Dalton was in his bed, all propped up with pillows and attempting to write in his journal.

"Hello there," he said. Angie smiled, and Billy ran to the foot of the bed to pet Sam.

"How are you feeling?" Angie asked.

"Terrible," Dalton said, closing his journal. "I'm glad your here."

Angie moved closer, and sat in the old rocking chair near the head of the bed. Dalton noticed she was carrying a nice camera.

"What's that you have there?"

"My camera," Angie said. "I was hoping—if you don't mind—to take some portraits of you; all this dramatic light, and shadows…"

"If that's what it takes to get you taking pictures again."

"Good," Angie smiled.

Meg yelled upstairs, "Billy, would you like some cookies and milk?"

"Yeah!" he said, and ran out of the room.

Hank barked and ran after him.

"Slow Down!" Angie said.

"Yes mom," Billy said as he ran down the stairs. Old Sam stretched and followed shortly behind them. Dalton handed Angie the white envelope from the night-stand.

"What's this?" Angie asked.

"Open it," Dalton said. She did and there were legal documents inside, without reading them closely she didn't understand what they were, but then she saw the check with her name on it—and gasped.

"What is this? I can't accept this," she said trying to hand it back to Dalton who grinned and wouldn't take it. "I can't take this Dalton."

"You will take it," Dalton said firmly. "Besides it's not all for you, this is for Billy as well. I want you to use some of that to buy a new car. This is more for my peace of mind. Please accept it." Dalton coughed into a handkerchief. "I want to know your not going to get stuck out there somewhere."

"It's too much," she said, looking down at the check.

"The other papers are for something I had my lawyer draw up, a trust fund for Billy. He can't touch it till he's eighteen, and I expect it to go towards college."

"Dalton, what about your family?"

"Look around, you can see how they're all flocking around." Dalton leaned his head back into his pillows. "I've lived modestly all these years, Meg's taken care of, and Dan, for the most part, will get what's coming to him. Angie, I think an awful lot of you. I want you to accept this graciously, and know that I wouldn't have done this if I didn't feel so strongly for you and Billy."

She nodded, stood up and hugged Dalton.

"Thank you," she said as her eyes filled with tears.

Meg and Billy came back into the room, followed by Hank, and finally Sam. They could tell that Angie had started to cry. Billy went straight to his mother, and Sam jumped up on the foot of the bed.

"What's wrong Mom?" Billy asked.

"I'm okay," she said. Billy looked confused, but Meg knew what they were talking about.

"I'll be downstairs," Meg said, and hurried out before she started to cry.

"Billy," Dalton said, "I have a couple problems I hope you can help me with."

"Sure," Billy said, leaning against the bed.

"Well, you see, before I got sick, I used to look after my sister Meg. She's old and all alone, and you see, I won't be around to look after her anymore. I was wondering if you might do that for me?" Billy looked at Angie, and she nodded yes through her tears.

"I can do that," Billy said.

"Good, I got one more *big* problem. It's this old cat, Sam. I guess he and I are like best friends…" Dalton tried to fight back the tears that welled up in his eyes. "I just can't take care of him anymore, and he really needs someone to feed him, and to look after him too." A tear rolled down Dalton's cheek, and over his lips. "Do you think you could take care of this old cat for me?"

Billy's eyes got real wide with excitement and looked to his mom again for approval. Again, she nodded yes.

"Sure!" Billy said, as Sam stepped over and rubbed against him, then rolled over onto his back.

"He seems to think a lot of you," Dalton said. "He doesn't act like that with anyone else." Billy smiled and was excited.

"Billy, there's one last thing," Dalton said. Billy looked up. "I just wanted you to know, that, if I would've ever had a grandson, I wish he could've been just like you."

Angie leaned over and took Dalton's hand, and Billy climbed up onto the bed and wrapped his little arms around Dalton's neck. Dalton closed his eyes—no longer fighting back the tears—he embraced Billy, and cried.

Forty-eight

Angie and Billy spent the entire afternoon with Meg while Dalton slept upstairs. Meg and Angie talked, and cried, and laughed as Billy rolled around on the floor with Hank. Old Sam observed the whole situation from the back of the couch.

At dusk Meg and Billy persuaded Sam into his cat-carrier, while Angie went out to warm up her car. Another vehicle turned into the driveway and slowly rolled over the frozen snow towards the house. Angie climbed out of her car as the other shut off it's headlights, and engine. Someone stepped out; it was Lilly.

Angie took a deep breath as Lilly walked up the driveway to her.

"Hello," Angie said. She could tell Lilly had been crying.

"Hello Angela," Lilly said.

"We're just getting ready to leave," Angie said. "I didn't know you were coming."

"Neither did I," said Lilly. There was an awkward silence between them. A cold breeze swayed the tall pines, casting dark shadows across the drive where they stood.

"Angela," Lilly said, "I'm sorry for being so hard on you."

There was another long silence, then Lilly stepped closer to Angie and awkwardly embraced her. Angie was frozen with confusion, but then returned the embrace.

Not long after Lilly's arrival, Angie, Billy left for home, along with a reluctant old Sam the cat. Meg cried as they drove away—she knew that old cat meant more to Dalton than he'd ever admit.

Meg and Lilly stood in the kitchen—and Meg embraced Lilly

again for the tenth time.

"I'm so glad your here," Meg said wiping away a tear with the corner of her apron, then reached for the teapot on the stove to fill it with water, "would you like some tea? You must be exhausted— that's such a long drive from the airport."

"No," Lilly said and stepped over to a bottle of whiskey on the counter-top. "But I'll have some of this."

"Oh," Meg said. "Well, sure."

"You don't mind?" Lilly asked, knowing Meg wasn't a drinker.

"Not at all," Meg said, and turned and to Lilly's surprise got two glasses out of the cupboard and set them on the counter-top.

Lilly poured, and Meg got some ice.

"None for me," Lilly said, "but thanks." Meg dropped all the ice into her glass. They moved over to the table and sat down across from one another. The house was quiet, and smelled of wood, and candles, and that evening's supper. Outside the wind had picked up, and over the ticking of the clock they could faintly hear the waves breaking onto the shore of Cathead Bay.

"To Dalton," Lilly said, and they lifted their glasses. Meg smiled and tears streamed down her cheeks, and they drank. Meg continued to sip hers. Lilly finished hers, and poured another. Meg wiped her tears away with her apron.

"Oh Lilly, I'm so glad your here".

Forty-nine

It was 3:47 P.M. and a week had passed since Lilly's arrival. She was asleep in the rocking chair next to Dalton's bed with Hank at her feet. Dalton had been writing in his journal, and had come to the end of the last sentence, on the last page. He put a period, signed his name, the date, and closed the journal. On the front cover he wrote 'For Dan,' then placed the journal on the night-stand next to his bed.

He watched Lilly sleep.

Eventually she woke up.

"You okay?" She asked.

"Yes," Dalton said.

"You've been watching me sleep?"

"Yes," Dalton said. She shook her head and looked across the room at the wedding photo still hanging on the wall.

"Why have you kept that hanging there all this time?" She asked.

"Your my wife."

"Come on Dalton, seriously."

"Well," Dalton said, looking so weak and feeble, "because through it all, you were the one. The one who always loved me, and that I truly loved. I put you through hell Lilly. I'm so sorry.

When we were married, I thought I was doing the best I could, but in hindsight, I know I wasn't, and was wrong. You loved me through so much, and I'll never know why you didn't leave me sooner."

"You old shit Dalton—*because I loved you!*" Lilly said, and leaned forward and took his frail hand. "I always loved you. I would have

walked through fire for you—for you to see what you were missing.
To see your son, to see me..."

"I was wrong Lilly. I wish I could go back. I wish I could do it all
over again—with you. The right way. I'm sorry."

"Oh *damn you* Dalton Jones," She said. She leaned to him, and
they gently embraced.

"I love you Lilly," Dalton whispered.

"I love you too," Lilly said.

Meg walked into the room, "I just about have dinner..." Meg
started to say, and saw Dalton and Lilly, and felt embarrassed that she
interrupted. Lilly sat up, still holding onto Dalton.

"I'm sorry," said Meg.

"Don't be," Lilly said, and Dalton waved Meg over to them,
and they opened their arms. They all embraced, and the ladies
began to cry.

"Oh for *Christ's sake!*" Dalton grumbled, and Lilly and Meg
laughed and wiped away their tears. Meg stood back up from sitting
on the edge of the bed and wiped her face with her apron.

"Well, what I came in here to tell you was that I have a pot roast
dinner ready, so you can eat when your hungry, if you can."

"Okay," Dalton said. "I'll try."

"I'm going to town now—are you sure you want me to go?"
Meg asked.

"Go Meg," Dalton said.

"Alright," said Meg, then she turned to Lilly for approval.

"We'll be fine," Lilly said.

"Alright. Well, I'll see you in a while," and she left the room
wiping her eyes again with the corner of her apron. They listened
to her walk down the stairs, shuffle around the kitchen, and out the
back door.

Lilly smiled and stood up slowly.

"Well, I'm starving," she said. "I'm going downstairs to get some
dinner. Do you need anything?"

"Yes, actually" Dalton said. "I need your help with something."

Lilly drew a hot bath, and went back to Dalton's bedroom. He was undressed and wearing his robe, sitting on the edge of the bed. Lilly went to him and helped him stand up. He put his arm around her neck to steady himself. They walked slowly through the bedroom and down the worn wood floors of the hall to the bathroom.

Lilly helped him take off his robe. She steadied him as he stepped into the tub of steaming water, and helped lower him down. The water burned, and distracted him some from the deep pain in his back and groin. Once he got into a comfortable position, Lilly let go.

"You okay?" She asked.

"Yeah," Dalton said. "Thank you."

Lilly stepped out of the bathroom, closed the door, and started back downstairs. As she passed his bedroom she stepped in and looked at their wedding portrait hanging slightly crooked on the wall. She reached up and straitened it, then quietly went downstairs.

In the bathroom, Dalton realized there was no whiskey bottle to tip back; he was actually relieved about that. Then he noticed the empty wooden stool next to the tub—it seemed odd without old Sam there.

Dalton had always thought of his life as if it were a novel—all the chapters, beginnings, and endings. If only reality was as perfect as fiction, and he could wrap up his life's story in a neat little package, avoiding the undesirable details of these final days; of sickness, pain, and ultimately his death. If Dalton's life were a novel—these moments would be a satisfying close—a perfect place to come to an end.

Made in the USA
Middletown, DE
30 June 2021